The Dark
Flight Down

Also by Marcus Sedgwick

THE BOOK OF DEAD DAYS
THE DARK HORSE
WITCH HILL
FLOODLAND

The Dark
Flight Down

Marcus Sedgwick

WENDY
LAMB
BOOKS

Published by
Wendy Lamb Books
an imprint of
Random House Children's Books
a division of Random House, Inc.
New York

Visit us on the Web! www.randomhouse.com/teens
Educators and librarians, for a variety of teaching tools, visit us at
www.randomhouse.com/teachers

Library of Congress Cataloging-in-Publication Data is available upon request.

ISBN: 0-385-74645-8 (trade)
0-385-90880-6 (lib. bdg.)

The text of this book is set in 12-point Goudy Old Style.
Printed in the United States of America
September 2005
10 9 8 7 6 5 4 3 2 1
BVG

For Pippa

Prologue

Midnight at the Imperial Court of Emperor Frederick III. The court has been emptied for the evening of its usual crowd of sycophants and entertainers, of its alchemists, astrologers, doctors, faith healers, druggists, noblemen, ne'er-do-wells, priests, actors and occultists.

The emperor sits on his throne, apparently alone, brooding. He lifts a pale hand, slowly, lazily.

"Maxim!" he calls, in his high, pathetic voice. "Dammit, Maxim, where are you?"

From the shadows behind the throne a tall, heavy figure emerges, swathed in a dark red robe that trails in the dust on the marble court floor. Maxim, the emperor's right hand, his confidant and oracle.

"Sire?" Maxim says. He is tired, but careful to show no sign of this to Frederick. He runs a hand across the top of his shaven head.

"There you are!" Frederick declares, but without emotion. "There you are."

"Sire," Maxim says, ready to do the emperor's bidding.

"Maxim, how many years have I left to live?"

Maxim hesitates briefly before answering, wondering how many times he has had this conversation with the emperor, and then, depressingly, he wonders how many *more* times he will have it.

"Sire, we have established beyond all possible doubt that you will live to a venerable age."

He bows, to try to emphasize the significance of his words, hoping they will be sufficient to keep Frederick happy.

"Yes, yes," says Frederick, far from happy. He lifts a long thin finger and scratches the side of his nose. Flakes of skin float into the gloom of the deserted court. "But how long? Exactly, would you say?"

Maxim sighs inwardly. It is not to be short, then.

"Ah!" he says brightly. "Well, our finest thinkers are convinced that you will live to be . . . a hundred!"

Frederick is silent for a while. Maxim begins to edge away.

"But what then?" Frederick cries suddenly.

Maxim hurries back to the foot of the throne.

"Well," he says. "Well! We have every right, every reason, to suppose that you will live to be a hundred and twenty. There is no reason why not."

"Ah. I see. One hundred. And twenty."

"Sire," says Maxim, wondering if he dare retire from the emperor's presence.

"But! But what then? What then, Maxim? What. Then."

Maxim is tired, and would very much like to be upstairs in his chambers, asleep, but he knows there is little chance of that now. Still he is careful to show no sign of his tiredness, his irritation.

2

"Sire, Your Excellency may then have the good grace to die."

That should shut him up, Maxim thinks, bowing his large frame as low as he can manage without falling onto his nose.

"Die?" Frederick whines. "Die? And what then?"

Maxim jerks his head upright, now irritated beyond reason by the emperor's voice.

"Well, sire," he says slowly, gazing at the ceiling, "there'll be . . . mourning. A period of great sorrow across the whole City. People will . . . stop to remember the great Frederick, and celebrate. They'll make . . ."

Maxim hesitates, inspiration deserting him. He looks down, and finds the emperor scowling at him.

"They'll make . . . ?"

"Yes, sire," says Maxim. "They'll make . . . boom boom."

"Boom boom?" Frederick asks. "They'll make boom boom? What in heaven's name do you mean? A celebration? Fireworks? Is that it? Is that all I will have to show for my time?"

Maxim lifts his head to the emperor, opens his hands wide and, for once, is at a loss for words.

Frederick rises to his feet. Even standing, his short, skinny frame remains dwarfed by his towering throne.

He points at Maxim.

"They will not make 'boom boom' because I am not going to die! Not ever. I will be one hundred, and then another one after that, and then another after that. Do you see, Maxim? Do you? I am the last of the line, Maxim, you know that as well as any. I have no kith, Maxim, no kin, no offspring, nor progeny. If I die, the chain is broken. The end is reached. The empire will have no emperor. There is only one answer. I am not going to die! You, my loyal servant, will see to it. I am not to die, and you are going to make sure of it."

Maxim hesitates. The old emperor is a fool. And he is a liar too. Some things cannot be forgotten, cannot be hidden as easily as Frederick would like, but Maxim doesn't dare tell him that.

"But, sire, I—"

"No, it is no use. I have made up my mind. Either you find a way to make me immortal, or your own end will be swifter than you might believe. Now get out of my sight, and find someone to carry me up to bed. You have no idea how bad it is for me, sitting on this throne all day."

"No, sire," says Maxim, his hand already pulling a bell-rope.

"And don't forget! Find a way to make me live forever. Or . . ."

And Maxim watches with a familiar prickle of horror as the feeble old emperor whisks a skinny finger across his own throat.

"*Phht!*"

The City

The Place of Obscured Memories

The City froze hard that winter, iron-cold and stone-still. When the snows came, they settled in to stay. It had started with snowstorms that seemed as if they were angry with something, as the wind whirled snowflakes down onto the City's filthy streets and crumbling buildings. It had started in the last few days of the year as Boy and Willow had been swept along by the magician Valerian in his ultimately futile quest for survival.

Then, early on New Year's Day, the fury abated, but still for day after day large fluffy flakes of pure whiteness drifted gently down, covering the muck and the mire, hiding the decay of the old City beneath a thick layer of pristine white youth.

The snow obliterated broken slates and chimney stacks, removed all traces of dilapidated walls and rotting windowsills and laid a clean and soft white carpet along every alley, street, avenue and parade, that was renewed every night.

It was as if the snow was trying to purify the squalid City, or at least hide its evil under a shroud of forgetting. Each night the old, horrible and grim was replaced by something new, young and beautiful.

But there was a price for this rebirth. It was cold, bitterly cold, and the City froze deep, and deathly still.

With it, something inside Boy froze too.

Too much had happened, too quickly.

Valerian. Boy couldn't even begin to think, to understand, about Valerian. He could barely feel.

He struggled to order, let alone comprehend, the events of the Dead Days, at the end of the year that had just died, taking his master Valerian with it. And beyond Valerian's death, there was what the scientist Kepler had said, right before the end. The thing that had tormented Boy's brain ever since, the truth of which still lay obscured.

That Valerian was Boy's father.

The new year that had just begun had hardly been a few hours old when Boy's one comfort had been taken from him too.

Willow.

2

"Come, Boy. It's time."

Boy turned for a moment from the window where he had been watching the snow fall. He had been trying to watch every single snowflake's path to earth, without knowing quite why he was doing it. He was almost obsessed. Every flake that fell hid the dark horror of the City a little more. Hid the horror, and dulled the memory. If it went on snowing, perhaps the horror would go too.

His attention drifted back to the snow.

"Boy!" said Kepler from the door. "It's time to go."

Boy turned to his new master again.

"Time for what?"

Kepler came into Boy's bedroom. It was a small room, simply furnished with a bed, a chair and a washstand, but after the tiny space he had slept in at Valerian's house, it was luxurious. Boy had not yet got used to it, and woke frequently through the night, feeling exposed, and vulnerable, as if death threatened. But maybe that had little to do with his new room.

Kepler joined him by the window, and put his skinny hand out to touch Boy's shoulder, but Boy flinched and pulled away. A scowl crossed Kepler's face as he drew back.

"For the funeral," he snapped. "You do still want to go to the funeral?"

Dumbly Boy nodded.

"Is it the fifth already?" he asked, but Kepler ignored him.

"I'll meet you in the hall in five minutes," he said, and left.

Boy was already watching the snow.

The fifth of January. Korp's funeral. Boy couldn't believe five days had already passed since Valerian had died.

There should be a funeral for him too, thought Boy.

But then, there was nothing to bury.

Just twenty more flakes, Boy said to himself, *then I'll get ready.* He watched the intricate dance that each flake made as it fell, trying to guess which way it would go, whether it would miss the top of the garden wall, or whether it would change direction at the last moment and make the foot of snow that capped the wall one flake thicker. After a while he began not merely to predict but to try to influence the journey of each flake, pushing with his mind into the frozen air outside his window, though he knew his imaginings were fanciful.

"Boy! It's time to go."

Boy dragged his gaze away from the window, grabbed his coat from back of the chair and ran to the door.

"I'm coming!" he called. He didn't want to miss the funeral. It wasn't so much that he wanted to bury Korp, the director of the theater where Valerian and Boy had performed. He had been murdered a few days before

Valerian's own demise. Boy had liked the fat old director well enough, and felt he should honor him by attending his funeral, but that was not really why he wanted to be there. He had spent enough time in graveyards recently to last a lifetime.

The real reason was Willow. Boy hoped she might be there too.

Five days had passed since he had seen her last, but those days had been a long clouded dream, in which he had struggled to control events and failed, unable to think or act clearly.

Kepler had sent her away.

Just a few hours after Valerian's death, Kepler had returned to them where they were still cowering in the ruined shell of Valerian's Tower room.

"Boy, you will work for me now," he had said. "I have made preparations. Go to my house. Wait for me there. Willow, come with me, I need your help."

But it had been a trick. He did not need Willow for anything other than to leave her somewhere and come back without her.

Boy had shouted at Kepler when he discovered what had happened. So timid and cowering around Valerian, Boy had found no trouble being angry with Kepler, no fear shouting at him.

"Bring her back!" he had screamed at his new master, who stood slowly shaking his head.

"You can't do this to us! Willow's all I've got now. Bring her back."

Kepler continued to shake his head.

"Wrong, Boy," he said. "You have me now. We will get to

know each other better. I need you, and Valerian has seen you are not wholly uneducated."

"Why do you need my help?"

Kepler hesitated. Boy didn't like it.

"I need your help. You'll help me with my plans. In time, we'll come to like each other. That's all you need to know for now."

"I don't . . . ," Boy had said, "I just want Willow. Why can't she live here too?"

"But don't worry, she is safe enough," Kepler went on. "She is working, so she will be able to look after herself. You need not think about her anymore."

"Tell me where she is!" Boy demanded. "Let me go to her!"

Boy had shouted and screamed, but Kepler had withstood it all, and left Boy to his own devices in his new bedroom.

Since that outburst, Boy had spent his time looking out the window, brooding. Trying to make sense of things that had no sense. That Valerian might have been his father all the while, without his knowing. And Kepler. Why did he want to keep Willow from him? Why did he think he needed Boy's help? Kepler was rich enough to employ a dozen assistants; why was Boy so special to him?

Answers refused to come, and as the days passed, Boy became hypnotized by the falling snow, which seemed to have no intention of stopping, ever.

Valerian had once told him that each snowflake was different from every other. Each with its own pattern, its own identity, and as they fell from the sky Boy discovered they each had their own behavior. No two fell in the same way.

Every one was unique, just, thought Boy, like people. And when the snowflake landed in the wrong place, on a warm roof, or a pond, it vanished instantly, gone forever. Its unique nature lost. Boy's thoughts turned again to Valerian, to Willow.

With a start he realized he couldn't clearly recall her face, even though they had only been separated for a few days. He had to force a memory of her delicate features and long hair into his mind, and was only satisfied when he could see her clearly again.

Now he ran down the stairs of Kepler's house and met his new master, who was waiting impatiently for him.

They set off into the City snowscape.

"Let's get on with it," Kepler said, irritably. "It's another freezing day and I don't want to waste it all perishing in some abysmal cemetery."

Boy kept pace with Kepler, dodging the larger drifts caught by corners and crevices, but still having to wade knee deep through snow in places. With every footstep, Boy crushed the identity from a thousand snowflakes, but he felt no pain for them.

His mind was on two things: Willow, and why Kepler wanted to keep them apart.

Within hours of Valerian's death Boy was under the control of Valerian's supposed friend Kepler. In reality Boy had discovered him to be Valerian's mortal enemy, to have contrived his death. It was a bitter history. At least to see Willow would remind him of sanity, of a kindness and care, even if she had no explanation for the madness of his world.

Though living in a haze since New Year, Boy could feel

new things starting to emerge in his mind. Like feeling something for Willow, maybe seeing things as they really were, and knowing that one day he might see his life with Valerian in a different light. He sensed that the real trouble with life always lay ahead—in the future, with all its traps and surprises and uncertainties, waiting to be faced. He supposed it was something to do with getting older.

The funeral was to be held in a small church, St. Hilary's, in the Quarter of the Arts, not far from the Old Theater, which had remained shut since Korp's murder. As Boy and Kepler made their way closer to the quarter, Boy suddenly realized something he had utterly forgotten. He was still wanted by the City Watch on suspicion for Korp's murder. So was Willow.

"Wait!" he said to Kepler.

"What is it, Boy?" Kepler asked, stopping. "We're going to be late at this rate. I didn't think the snow was this bad."

"The Watch. Supposing they come to the funeral—looking for Willow and me?"

"You need not fear," said Kepler. "I've been asking around. They've changed their tack. They think it was the Phantom who murdered Korp. When they stopped to think about it, they saw lots of similarities between his murder and those of other victims. The excessive force. The considerable blood loss. Not something you or Willow could have done."

Boy was only partially reassured. In his experience the Watch were a dim-witted lot, who could easily believe anything that came into their heads from one minute to the next. But it was worth the risk of being arrested, if it meant seeing Willow.

14

They were at the end of a narrow lane that opened into a small square called Well Court, at the far end of which Boy saw the side of St. Hilary's. It looked as if the church had been squeezed in among the gaggle of taller buildings that surrounded it, though in fact the church had been there first. They skirted the church wall and came to the small churchyard that lay beyond. People were gathering round a hard-dug hole in the frozen ground. The snow continued to fall. The funeral was about to begin.

3

More people than Boy expected turned up for Korp's funeral. There were many of his old friends from the theater, the musicians, the stagehands and costume girls. He gazed around at the faces of all the performers and musicians and actors who had come to pay their respects to the old director. He tried to guess who they were, and what they were, singers or jugglers, or maybe, like Valerian, there was a magician among them. No, there was no one like Valerian. There could never be a magician like Valerian. Valerian, whose magic was sometimes just stage trickery, and sometimes . . . sometimes something more.

Boy saw a small old lady at the front of the crowd with a fluffy dog on a lead. It took him a moment to remember she was Korp's housekeeper. She had brought Korp's faithful dog, Lily, with her. There was Snake-girl, looking quite plain without her snake. Boy realized only now that her snake and her costume were what made her seem so mysterious and alluring. It was like a new kind of vision, seeing with eyes as keen as scalpel blades, that cut away desires and emotions and wishful thinking and left only what was fact. It hurt, sometimes, if you looked upon the wrong thing, and it could burn. Not seeing Willow among the many still arriving for Korp's funeral, he turned his face to the sky and watched the hundreds upon thousands of huge feathery snowflakes fall into the churchyard.

Now Boy noticed something else. People were looking at him, nudging each other and pointing at him with a nod of their heads. As he caught their eye they'd look away, and Boy soon heard enough of a whisper to know what it was. Valerian. Here was Valerian's boy, somehow still alive despite the rumors that both he and Valerian had perished in some awful, occult cataclysm in the Yellow House on New Year's Eve.

"Ignore them," Kepler said quietly.

News traveled fast, and rumor and gossip even faster. Yes, Valerian was dead, but that was only half the story. Boy had survived, after all. The crowds stared at him. He looked thinner than ever, his pale skin ghostlike and gray, but he was nonetheless alive.

And what would they think, Boy thought bitterly, *if they knew the rest of it? That Valerian was my father.*

Kepler had said so, and then denied it almost as soon as he had uttered the words.

It seemed so unreal to Boy, the Boy who was finally seeing what was truth and what was untruth. Maybe he'd just imagined Kepler had said it. Those last few minutes before Valerian had gone had been so chaotic: the noise, the light, the wind in the Tower. Maybe he'd just wanted to hear what he thought Kepler had said, and had imagined it.

But no. Kepler had told Valerian that he was Boy's

4

Willow stood on the far side of the grave, hidden from the waist down by the pile of earth spoil that would soon be covering Korp's coffin. Boy made to move toward her, but there was Kepler's hand on his shoulder immediately.

"Have some respect, Boy."

Kepler nodded to where the pallbearers were making their way through the crowd.

The ceremony began and ended and finally they shoveled some of the earth back into the hole, hiding the coffin as the City was being hidden by snow. Hiding it from sight, as if that could hide it from memory.

Boy knew there was something wrong with what he was watching, but couldn't place what it was. Korp's dog, Lily, however, could. As the frozen clods of earth began to drum onto the wood of the coffin lid, the sad little mutt shivered and then began to let out a pathetic whimper. She knew that simply because something was gone from sight did not mean it was gone from memory, and she missed her master.

The snow fell, and Boy shut his mind to everything but its falling.

Now he knew what was strange about the funeral. All these people were united by the one thing that wasn't there: the dead. It was the first funeral Boy had ever been to, and it struck him as profoundly strange.

Korp was not the only person missed by the mourners. It seemed strange that Valerian was not there too. As people started to drift away, Boy looked across the gathering, and caught a glimpse of a tall figure in black striding along the street. For a second he thought it was his dead master come back to life.

It was only a priest hurrying through the snow.

Suddenly the old violinist who had often been kind to Boy clapped his hands.

"Wait! We cannot leave it at that! Will you join me, friends, in celebrating the life of our dear director?"

People murmured and nodded.

"Quite so!" someone called.

"To the Feather, then?" the violinist said. "The first drinks are on me!"

Boy had lost sight of Willow, then saw her through the crowd, beckoning him.

"Can we go?" Boy asked Kepler. "Can we go to the Feather?"

"No," said Kepler. "We've done what we came to do."

But before they could move, the old violinist, Georg, and a couple of his friends came over to where Boy and Kepler stood. Without a glance at Kepler, they fussed over Boy, walking him away from the grave, along with everyone else heading for the tavern, and Kepler could do

nothing but follow, hopping at their heels like an un-
wanted dog.

Boy could feel his feet again. Somewhere in the crowd of
people up ahead was Willow. That in itself gave Boy
warmth.

5

"So you're the boy's new master?"

Now Boy and Kepler found themselves sitting squashed around a table in the filthy tavern called the Feather. Talk quickly moved from the uncertain future of the theater to Valerian, and then to Boy. Boy watched, squirming un-easily while Georg and the others questioned Kepler. Willow was nearby, picking greedily at a bowl of intensely sweet raisins in the middle of the table. She glanced over at Boy, smiling.

Kepler saw this.

"We must go. Boy and I have work to do," he said for the fourth time in as many minutes, but no one got up to let him out.

A large man on Kepler's left smiled at Boy.

"Run and fetch the barmaid, will you? More drinks all round."

"And get her to bring some absinthe, eh? A game of snapdragon, anyone? Korp would have loved that!"

There was a loud cheer round the table as Boy pushed his way through to find the barmaid, trying to catch Willow's eye as he left.

By the time he got back, they'd already found a bottle of

absinthe somewhere else. They had dispensed with beer in favor of this devilish green liquor, and had embarked upon a game of snapdragon.

Boy loved this game, largely because he usually got away without having to play himself, just watching as others fell off their chairs from the drink. He almost felt sorry for Kepler, who had obviously never heard of snapdragon before, and was about to learn all about it the hard way.

"Right," Georg was saying to Kepler, "now you know how to play, let's do it properly."

On the table was a small saucer into which a little of the absinthe had been poured. A handful of raisins was added. The game was to pick up a raisin from the saucer and eat it. If you succeeded, the play moved round to the next person at the table. If you dropped the raisin, you had to sink a glass of the drink.

"What do you mean, properly?" Kepler asked Georg.

"Well, that time we were just showing you how it's played. Now we're going to do it properly. Wilfred? Will you?"

And Wilfred, the strong man, took a box of matches from his pocket, and set light to the absinthe.

"You can start," Wilfred said, smiling at Kepler.

"What? But it's burning!"

"Well, it wouldn't be much of a game if it wasn't," Georg said, nudging Wilfred, who started chuckling.

Kepler stared nervously around him, then at the saucer of burning raisins and absinthe. He darted his hand to the flames. He managed to pick one up, but dropped it on the table with a squeal and sucked his burned fingers.

Everyone roared with laughter, and Wilfred shoved a

glass of absinthe under his nose. Kepler looked at it miserably, then, with the strong man glaring at him, took a sip.

"Not like that!" Wilfred cried, and pulling Kepler's nose back, tipped the whole lot down his open mouth.

Everyone hooted with laughter again, and play moved round to Wilfred, who deftly snatched a raisin and popped it into his mouth in a single motion.

"Doesn't it burn your fingers?" said a voice beside Boy, and there at last was Willow.

Boy smiled and for a moment didn't know what to do or say. He simply stared into her eyes, her face for once not framed by her hair, which she had pulled back into a bunch.

"Or your mouth, come to that," Willow added, staring as Georg took two at once, and flicked them into his mouth with professional skill.

"Not if you do it quickly," Boy replied. "And shut your mouth as soon as it's in. I watched Valerian play this hundreds of times. He always won. It amused him, and he'd win money too, sometimes. There'd be everyone else drinking their heads off, and he'd just sit watching them."

Willow laughed, and without thinking, Boy laughed too.

"I used to pick their pockets if I thought Valerian wasn't watching!"

"Boy!" said Willow. "You are bad!"

"It meant I could buy something extra to eat . . . ," Boy said defensively, but then saw Willow was only teasing.

The game was getting noisier. Kepler tried to make one more attempt to leave, but Boy could see he was very drunk, and he fell back in his chair without anyone's even making him stay this time.

"Valerian could do it slowly, though, too," Boy said. "When everyone was really drunk, he'd start to show off. He could pick one up ever so slowly, with his fingertips right in the fire, and slowly put the raisin on his tongue, and let it burn there for a bit, as if it wasn't hurting at all. I don't know how he did that."

Willow shrugged.

"Maybe he was just good at controlling pain."

Boy said nothing, lost in memories.

Controlling pain, he thought.

He roused himself and looked at Willow. She looked well enough. It had only been five days, but it felt like months.

"Willow . . . ?"

"I'm all right. He took me to an orphanage. I thought just to live there, but he's got me a job. I didn't like the idea at first, but it's much nicer than the one I grew up in. I'll even get paid! I sneaked out today. I'll probably be in trouble, but it won't be bad. There's a woman who's in charge. She's quite fierce, but I think she's soft enough underneath. She's called Martha."

Boy stared at Willow, at her long brown hair and wax white face. He put his hand out to her cheek, and she took it away gently and held it in hers.

"How are you, Boy?" she said softly. "Is he all right with you?"

Boy wondered whom she meant, then realized she was talking about Kepler.

"Yes. He feeds me. And doesn't shout at me, and doesn't beat me, or even get cross with me. It's fine."

"But what are you doing?"

"Nothing. He says he needs me to help him, but we've done nothing. I just sit in my room. I've been watching the snow, Willow. There's so much of it. So much snow. It's hard to recognize some bits of the City. Have you seen? Just so much snow."

Willow looked at Boy, a frown on her face. Then she forced a smile.

"Will you stay with him?" she asked.

Boy shrugged.

"I don't know. I suppose so. I don't want to go back to the streets, even living with Valerian was better than that, and . . ."

He stopped.

"What is it?" Willow asked.

"Willow. What Kepler said. You remember?"

"That Valerian was your father? Yes."

"Tell me. Tell me honestly. Do you think it's true?"

Willow tried to look down and away, but Boy wouldn't let her.

"I don't know," she said, finally.

Boy said nothing.

"Would it change anything? Would it change how you felt about him, if he was? Would it change how you felt about how he treated you? Or that he's dead?"

Boy shrugged and looked away.

"Let him go, Boy," she said. "Let him go, and let yourself go too. You've got a new life to start."

Boy turned back to her.

"Have I? With Kepler?"

"No," said Willow. "I thought . . . I thought with me."

She spoke quickly, not giving Boy a chance to interrupt.

26

"I've got a proper job now. Imagine that. I'll have money! We could find somewhere to live. Maybe you could find work too. We could go to another part of the City, where Kepler would never find you. Maybe we could even leave the City itself. . . ."

She stopped, biting her lower lip.

"But maybe you don't—"

"Yes," said Boy. "Yes, Willow, I do."

Willow flung her arms around him and they both began to cry, while beside them the snapdragon got louder and louder and more drunken with every round.

Willow and Boy knew nothing of this, as they talked and talked and quietly began to make plans for themselves. It felt strange to both of them; that they could decide what to do with their lives, not have them dictated by other people.

When they finally stopped talking, only Georg and Wilfred were left sitting at the table.

"Where's . . . ?" Boy asked, openmouthed.

"Your Mr. Kepler?" Georg asked. He pointed a finger at the floor.

Leaning over in his chair, Boy looked under the table to see Kepler asleep on the floor.

"I'd better get him home," Boy said. "He'll get himself slit if he stays here."

"Well, there's one thing at least," Georg said to Boy.

"What's that?"

"Your master will be kinder to you tomorrow."

"Why?" asked Willow.

"Well," said Georg, winking at Wilfred, "everyone knows. Absinthe makes the heart grow fonder!"

And he and Wilfred burst into fits of drunken giggles at what was obviously a joke they'd told many, many times.

Boy frowned.

"Don't fret," said Wilfred to Boy, still chuckling. "I'll carry him for you, if you show me the way."

"You can trust him," said Georg. "He's my good friend, and there's no way you can carry your master, is there?"

Boy smiled.

"You're right. Thank you," he said. "For everything."

Georg tipped his hat to Boy and Willow, and made to leave himself. Wilfred knelt down beside Kepler and swung his sagging body up onto his shoulder.

"He'll have a head tomorrow," he said.

Boy looked at Willow.

"So, I'll see you tomorrow evening. By St. Valentine's Fountain?"

Willow nodded, smiling. She skipped forward, kissed Boy quickly on the lips and ran off.

Boy led the way back to Kepler's house. Wilfred was silent and Boy was happy for it to be so, because all he wanted to do was think about Willow.

He thought about what he knew about her. It seemed he knew very little. That she had been born in the country-side but had been orphaned when she was tiny. She had lived in an orphanage, had worked for the City Liverymen and had then come to the theater. That was really all he knew, and he felt it was out of balance with how much they had gone through together in the preceding few days. It was from those experiences that he really knew who Willow was, what she was. Strong, brave and kind. With a shock Boy realized that although he knew very little of

Willow's life, he still knew more about her history than he did about his own.

As he went he kept himself warm with the memory of the fleeting kiss and the thought that from tomorrow he and Willow would be together for good.

Nothing could have been further from the truth.

6

Boy got to bed around three in the morning, having first seen that his master was safely asleep.

Wilfred had taken Kepler upstairs and tipped him onto the mattress, then tipped his hat just as easily to Boy, and turned to go.

"Strange dreams for him tonight," Wilfred had chuckled.

Boy looked at him quizzically.

"The absinthe." He winked, and went.

Boy considered Kepler for a while, then decided he was too tired to do anything much for him. He pulled Kepler's boots off and drew a coverlet up to his chin.

Boy slept late into the morning, and if Kepler's dreams were strange, then Boy's were every bit as disturbing. When Boy woke finally, it was with no gentle arousal, but with a lurch and a jolt as his dream frightened him awake. He sat up in bed for several minutes, breathing hard, trying to calm down. It had been a long time since he had dreamed at all, he realized. As if to make up for that, he had been ridden into the ground by a stampede of nightmares.

Almost automatically Boy thought of snow as he swung his legs over the side of the bed. His dreams had been frozen like mountain snow, and with a sudden warm spell had thawed, sending a deluge of meltwater cascading down on him.

Dreams still lay in his mind like a fog as he staggered over to the washstand and splashed icy water into the bowl from the jug beside it. He had been in a dark space, a small dark space. That was not the frightening part. Not for Boy. Small dark spaces were where he felt safest, as he had grown up on the streets, and later with Valerian too. They had always been good places for him.

Having stolen a purse or a loaf, anywhere he could tuck his narrow bones to hide from the Watch was good for Boy; a tiny crevice in a church roof was heaven. Being with Valerian onstage, tucked into magical cabinets and other boxes, was at least one time when his master could not beat him or curse him. And, in the Yellow House, Boy's room had been that narrow triangular tunnel, too small even to stand in, but a place of safety nonetheless.

So it wasn't the small dark space in his dream that had been scary, but something else. Something lurking nearby. Something that breathed with a low, husky rattle, like a creature being half throttled. Some sort of fiend.

Boy remembered the dream and cursed it, for it signaled an end to his view of darkness as a benevolent thing. He plunged his face into the cold water in the bowl in front of him, and held it there, opening his eyes, so the water washed them, hoping it would wash the black clouds from his brain too.

But it did not. He was starting to fully feel the shock of all that had happened in the Dead Days. He stood upright again, breathing hard, knowing that the safety of darkness had already long gone. It had not just vanished with the previous night's dream of some foul monster in the dark. It had died in those vile underground tunnels when he had been hunted by Valerian, his former master. His father?

Boy dressed and stood in front of the window. Outside, the snow was falling as heavily as it ever had over the last week. Boy tried his trick of watching the snow, to hypnotize himself into forgetting, but it failed.

His dreams had unlocked his emotions, the fear jerking him from the stupor of the previous few days. And this flood of emotions had unleashed another dreadful realization. He knew he had to find out the truth about Valerian, one way or the other. Not knowing had been tormenting him, he saw that clearly now, and he had to put a stop to it.

He knew how to do it. He himself had helped provide the answer to his problem.

The book. The magical book Valerian had sought. It contained answers, truths and secrets, and the histories and destinies of any who dared to read its pages. It had enlightened some, but had fooled many more, for its answers were not always clear and precise. The book revealed something of its readers' fates, but Boy had already learnt that Fortune was a fickle mistress, largely because people saw only what it suited them to see.

Nonetheless, the book itself was all-knowing, as Boy was only too aware. He and Willow had helped Valerian hunt down the book, only to find that Kepler already had it, and, ensnared by its power, was trying to keep it from Valerian.

If Boy was going to look in the book, now was the time

to do it, while Kepler slept off his absinthe-curdled dreams. The enormity of what he had decided to do dawned on him, and his heart began to pound.

Something else occurred to Boy. The book would also be able to tell him another thing, something he desperately wanted to know, and which no one and nothing else would ever be able to tell him.

His real name.

7

The house was quiet. The whole City felt quiet, as if everyone and everything in it were watching offstage, as Boy crept down the corridor from his room.

Words came into Boy's head, from nowhere. They felt familiar, though he couldn't work out why. It was true that the snowfall had been hypnotizing him, helping him bury his troubles, but if some parts of his memory were being hidden, at the same time he had become strangely awake to others.

"Surely you won't run, when your boat is ready to sail."

He pushed the words to the back of his mind, but they would not disappear.

"Surely you will stay and face the gentle rain."

He couldn't place the words, and tried again to ignore them.

Now he drew even with Kepler's door, and paused, on tiptoe. He held his boots in his hands, not daring to risk booted footsteps on the bare wooden boards of the corridor.

Boy held his breath, straining to hear any sound from Kepler, any noise that might show he was stirring. All was quiet.

Boy breathed out and headed for the top of the stairs.

A first doubt rose in his mind. It wasn't conscience, but fear. He had no qualms about looking at the book, which he supposed now belonged to Kepler. He had stolen enough things in his life not to worry about borrowing something without permission. No, that was not the cause of his doubt. The cause was fear.

Sitting on the last stair, he pulled his boots on. The floor was carpeted here, and he was no longer scared about Kepler's hearing him. What he was scared of lay, he assumed, in front of him, in Kepler's study, where he had last seen Kepler put the book.

Boy crossed the hall, and the rogue words pushed into his head again.

"Surely you won't run . . . ?"

Willow had thought the book dangerous. He knew that much from the brief time they had spent together before Valerian's end on New Year's Eve. Why else would its owners, the Beebe family, have buried it in a tomb with their son, Gad, its last owner, if it were not dangerous? It had lain undisturbed in his grave in the church at Linden until Kepler had located it, and stolen it. At first Boy hadn't understood how a book could be dangerous, but he now knew enough to make him nervous. The book was unadulterated knowledge, pure and powerful.

Boy reached the study door, and put his finger to the brass knob. The house was cold; he had lit no fires, and with no one else to do it, it would remain that way. He shivered, but turned the knob and pushed the door open.

Quickly he stepped inside and gently pushed the door to behind him, without risking making any noise by closing it properly.

He looked at the desk. Unless Kepler had moved it, the book lay inside the bottom drawer on the right-hand side, waiting.

The thing was just to do it, without thinking, without worrying. Boy thought of snowfall and took seven short strides over to the desk.

He sat down in the leather-covered chair and looked at the drawer. It would be locked, Boy knew that, and Kepler had the only key, but that was no problem for Boy. He rummaged in his pocket and pulled out the bent piece of metal that he used to pick locks. It had belonged to a metal hand that Kepler had once dissected with Valerian, and it had been Valerian who had shown Boy how to pick locks. So, he reasoned, they only had themselves to blame.

He leant down to the lock of the bottom drawer, and twisted the metal around inside, feeling for the tumblers.

Boy usually sprang a lock in a few moments, but he was not surprised that Kepler, a man of invention and mechanism, should have superior devices to secure his property. The lock resisted.

Boy got out of the chair and knelt down at eye level with the lock, determined not to be beaten.

On the other side of a finger's width of oak lay the book, waiting to tell Boy everything.

He jiggled the metal pin inside the lock once more. He struggled with the lock frantically. He could sense the book only inches away, could sense its power, but the lock defeated all his attempts to open it.

He sat back in the chair, angry now, and kicked the desk.

He looked around, and his eyes rested on the fireplace. There was a heavy iron poker by the grate.

Boy stood.

He would smash the stupid desk apart, and take the book. He and Willow had agreed to meet by the fountain later that day, and so he would, but with the knowledge of his past and his future revealed. Kepler would be angry, but that wouldn't matter—Boy would never see him again.

Boy reached the fireplace and grasped the poker by its twisted handle.

As he turned to make for the desk, the door swung open, and Kepler walked in.

For a second a hateful vision of violence passed through Boy's mind, as he saw himself bringing the poker down on Kepler's head, spilling his brains onto the red carpet of the study floor.

But it was gone in an instant. If anyone was in the *mood* for violence, it was Kepler. No doubt as a result of the absinthe, he was in a strange frame of mind. Boy saw the turmoil in his master's eyes, and the sudden craving he had felt for the book disappeared. Boy had seen absinthe do this to people before. Normally calm people might practically murder each other when recovering from the strange hallucinations that the wormwood-ridden drink could induce.

"Boy!" Kepler snapped. "It's perishing cold. Why aren't the fires lit?"

"I'm just doing them," Boy said quickly, waving the poker. "The house will be warm soon."

Kepler ignored him, and staggered to the desk, where he sat in the chair. He was too hung over to notice either that Boy was poking a fire that had not yet been lit, or that the papers on his desk and the chair were not where he'd left them.

"You are not to see those people again," said Kepler. He meant Georg and the others from the theater.

Boy was about to argue, but thought better of it. He would be gone by this evening, and what Kepler thought or said would not matter. He could be angry about it then, could laugh about it then, so for now he just nodded and went on preparing the fire.

"I need you to do something for me," said Kepler thickly. "I need you to fetch something for me, this morning."

Boy stood and looked at Kepler, whose head was still in his hands. Now he lifted it, but slowly.

"I need you to fetch something for me, from the Yellow House."

Boy froze. The Yellow House. Valerian's house.

"I—" began Boy, but Kepler was in no mood to argue.

"Just go," he said. "I need a lens from the camera. It's the only one of its kind in the City, and cost a fortune. I want it back. I built that thing, it belongs to me now Valerian's gone. I want it to project an image. . . ."

Boy wondered what he was talking about, but said nothing.

"You must unscrew the bottom section of the brass tube and the lens will drop out. Don't break it! And come straight back."

Boy was used to being told what to do. It was all he had ever had from Valerian. He would help Kepler with this last thing. It wouldn't take very long, and anyway he would have to wait now for another chance to look at the book. Once he had, he could disappear to be with Willow.

Kepler had saved his life, after all, by sending Valerian to his death, instead of Valerian sending Boy to his. He decided he owed the man one favor at least, but there was something else too. He wanted to go to the Yellow House one more time, to see what had become of where he had lived with Valerian all those years. Maybe, in some way, to say goodbye.

He put on his coat and made for the door, leaving Kepler clutching his head.

The Yellow House

The Place of Broken Futures

1

The new year was not quite a week old. Life in the City was not yet in full swing; it was a quiet time of year anyway, but people seemed to be using the endless snow as an excuse for doing as little as possible.

Boy turned into a squalid and narrow street called Three Horse Run to find it empty of its usual loiterers and layabouts, and as he made his way along it, his were the first footsteps that broke the snow's perfection.

Everywhere was the same; he saw barely half a dozen souls as he headed for the place he knew so well, the Yellow House. Despite Kepler's insistence that the men of the Watch were no longer after Boy, he retained his instinct to go unnoticed wherever possible, and was glad of the empty streets.

Finally, as he made his way down Salted Frog Alley, he heard voices approaching. He looked up and saw three costermongers wheeling a barrow of vegetables slowly through the snow. Relieved that they were not Watchmen, Boy nonetheless still had no desire to see or talk to anyone, and pressed himself into a deep doorway at the side of the alley.

He waited as they passed. They were deep in conversation and didn't notice Boy, but even if they'd been looking for him they would probably have missed him, he was so good at hiding.

Boy heard snatches of their conversation.

". . . all over the street . . ."

". . . couldn't even tell who it was. Poor blighter!"

"They said the snow was turned red for two hundred yards. This great long trail. Then it stopped at a gutter by the river."

"I heard the blood was sprayed everywhere, like a firework."

Boy shuddered. He knew what they were talking about.

"Bits of the body were missing, that's for sure. The same as the others."

"Nonsense!" said another. "It's the blood it's after. The Phantom can't be seen or killed. It won't be stopped."

"You're both exaggerating. It's just some lunatic on the loose."

His friend spat in the snow as they passed near Boy.

"Maybe. But whatever it is, it's still killing for fun, isn't it? The Watch have no idea what to do."

Boy shrank back in the doorway. The Phantom had killed again.

It was around one in the afternoon when Boy turned the corner of Blind Man's Stick and there was the Yellow House, looking the same as it always did apart from the snow covering its roofs: tall and imposing, but faded and in need of repair.

Boy couldn't help lifting his eyes to the very top of the house, to the Tower, where it had all ended for Valerian. It was a bizarre addition to the rambling house, showing no sign of the horrors that had unfolded there on New Year's Eve. Inside it lay the camera, and the lens that Kepler wanted. Boy would have to face his memories.

He still had the key to the house that Valerian had given him only a few days before, on Childermas, the unluckiest day of the year. Well, the key was one piece of good luck, Boy thought, as he rattled it in the lock of the outer gates.

He had to force the heavy iron gates away from him through the deep snow and squeeze through. Now he opened the door to the house itself.

From force of habit he checked to see that no one had seen him enter. Then Boy stepped into the hall and closed the door behind him.

It had been only six days since anyone had been there, but the Yellow House had already acquired that strange eerie silence that houses gather about themselves when left alone for any length of time.

"Hello?" Boy said quietly into the air around him, then felt faintly stupid for doing so. Of course there was no one there. There had been no one there since the early hours of the new year, when Kepler had come back for him and Willow.

He made his way upstairs to the third-floor landing. From there he could have gone along to where the ladder led up to his little room, but he didn't want to see it.

Only six days, but it felt like an eternity had passed. He

45

couldn't believe the house was so still, so empty, so big. Had it always been like this? Maybe he just hadn't noticed, when Valerian had been there issuing orders and threats in equal measure.

He turned his back on the corridor and headed for the foot of the spiral staircase that led to the Tower. As he made his way up he could already see the remains of the shattered door where Kepler and Willow had burst in to save him from Valerian. Just the sight of the fractured wood made Boy panic, as a rush of memories rose unbidden in his mind.

He tried to concentrate on what he had come to do, but as he stepped over the threshold into the room itself, the events of New Year's Eve overwhelmed him and he sank to the floor, weak and shaking.

He shook his head, trying to clear it.

"The lens," he said aloud, as if the sound of his voice could dispel the demons lurking in the room. "Just get the lens and go."

He looked up.

The room was a mess. They had left it exactly as it was after the awful cataclysm, the wind, the apparition. The hundreds upon hundreds of Valerian's books lay in chaotic heaps across the floor, various papers and parchments strewn over them. Even the trapdoor in the middle of the room was covered in books and papers. Valerian's great leather armchair lay on its side. Broken glass and tangled metal from his experimental equipment lay in confusion across the tabletops. The only thing that seemed unharmed was the camera obscura itself. The shutters were drawn, and in the half darkness of the room, Boy saw that the camera was still working. Kepler had warned Valerian that it would be of no use in saving his skin, but he had built a good machine, and it worked still, projecting a curved but clear image of the streets outside onto the circular white tabletop beneath it.

Boy scrambled over to it, passing the upturned armchair as he did. He paused, and then pulled Valerian's favorite chair back onto its feet.

"That's better," he said, and smiled as he remembered Valerian sitting in it.

He turned to the camera. At the base that overhung the table was a wide brass cylinder. From this the image poured onto the table. He supposed this was what Kepler had been talking about, so he climbed onto the tabletop and lay looking up at the apparatus.

He pushed and pulled the thing, and could see no way of loosening it, but then remembered what Kepler had said about unscrewing it, and he began to twist. Immediately it turned, opening a join that was so finely wrought it had been invisible before the thread began to unwind.

Boy twisted some more, and the bottom half of the cylinder came away from the top. As it did, he suddenly recalled what Kepler had warned about breaking the glass lens, and slid underneath the projection device. The image of the City outside was now played out on Boy's face and chest, and had there been anyone there to see, and had they looked closely, they would have seen snow falling across him. It fell across his eyes and face, but unlike the snow falling outside, which gathered in piles, the flake after flake after flake that crossed Boy's face kept on falling, but hid no horror.

47

He nearly had it apart now, and chewed his lip as he lowered the bottom half of brass away from the top.

"Hold hard there, you brat!" said a voice from the door, and Boy jerked upright, hitting his head on the camera. He clutched the lens as he swung down to the floor.

"I said hold!"

2

At first Boy thought he faced men of the City Watch. Three figures stood in the doorway, but now he noticed their uniforms were not the black of the Watch; they wore the dark gray garb of the Imperial Guard. If there was any doubt over this, the white feathers on their helmets confirmed it; Watchmen wore either red or pink. Only the Imperial Guard wore white.

"Looting? That your game, boy?"

The leader stepped forward.

"Give that to me," he said, indicating the lens in Boy's hand.

For a moment, Boy was too stunned to say anything; then he remembered where he was.

"No," said Boy. "I'm not stealing. I live here."

This seemed to throw the guard.

"What do you mean you live here? This is the house of Valerian, the magician. Now deceased, we understand. No one else lives here."

"That's not true!" Boy cried. "I do. I've lived here for years. I'm Valerian's boy."

"His son? He has no son! Don't make a fool of me, boy."

"No, not his son. That is, I'm not sure. . . ."

At this all three of the guards laughed and began to move toward Boy.

"You're not sure!" said the leader. "You lived here for years and you don't know if you're really his son or not? I'll tell you what, you rascal! You are a thief. Now get out of here, we have serious business to attend to."

"No," shouted Boy, "you get out of here. This is Valerian's house, and yes, he's dead. But I live here and this place belongs to me if it belongs to anyone! I was his boy!"

Now the leader of the guards looked at his two men, then back at Boy.

"You say you were his?"

Boy nodded.

"I lived here and worked for him. I was his assistant."

"Right, then, you're coming with us. We have orders to remove all articles belonging to Valerian, and if you were his boy then that includes you."

Boy laughed nervously.

"You don't really mean that, do you?"

"Don't give us trouble, now. You can't get away. It will be easier for all of us if you just come along with us to the palace."

"The palace?" Boy spluttered. "You can't!"

"I've had enough of this," the guard said to his men. "Get him out of my sight."

And with that the two other Imperial Guards made for Boy.

"No!" cried Boy. He glanced at the guards, then leapt to

the wall where the release for the trapdoor lay. He pulled the lever and the floor opened up between the guards and himself, shedding books and papers that tumbled down into the air.

The guards, surprised for a moment, smiled when they looked down through the trapdoor and saw the perilous drop not to the third- but the second-floor landing, a leg-breaking fall.

"That's not going to help you!"

"We'll see," said Boy, and shoving the lens into his coat pocket, he launched himself for the gap, catching hold of the winch rope that was used to hoist things up to the Tower.

He had gambled that it would unwind slowly enough to break his fall somewhat, and because of his slight frame, it worked. He landed on the second floor with a thump, but nothing bad enough to stop him.

"Get him!" cried a voice from above.

Boy scrambled to his feet, briefly glancing up. The guards peered down at him. The end of the hoist rope had freed itself from the pulley and fell around Boy's legs.

"Don't just gawp at him! After him! The stairs!"

Boy leapt for the stairs, taking them three at a time. As he made the ground floor he felt safe. He could hear the guards lumbering along the second-floor landing. He sprinted across the hall for the door, and then something tangled his legs and he went sprawling along the stone floor, jarring his wrist as he fell. He looked to see what had caught him, and glimpsed one of the guards leaning over the banister. He had thrown the winch rope in a bundle, which had snagged Boy's calves as he ran.

Footsteps thudded closer. Boy struggled to his feet and pulled at the front door.

He flung it open and ran straight into a fourth guard, waiting there for such an event. The guard was surprised and took a second to react. Boy tried to sidestep him, but it was too late.

First one, then two pairs of hands pulled him back and wrestled him to the ground.

"Right! You little swine," said the guard. "You're coming to the palace."

They brought the rope and tied his arms behind him and then his legs, leaving him trussed up like a slaughtered deer.

None of them saw the lens fall from Boy's pocket and roll a little way into the snow.

Outside in the street was a cart attached to a sturdy-looking horse. Boy was the first of Valerian's possessions to be thrown into it, and while one of the guards waited with him, the other three spent the afternoon loading alongside him anything from the Tower room that wasn't bolted down.

Darkness had fallen when the cart finally set off at walking pace. Boy lay uncomfortably on his side, half covered by Valerian's books and other possessions. His arms and legs had gone numb hours before, and it was all he could do to keep one eye on where they were going. After a while he gave up, and tried to ask the guards what they were going to do with him.

They did not reply.

"Please," pleaded Boy, "at least tell me where we're going."

One of them turned round and grunted.

"We told you. The palace. You belong to the emperor now."

3

Willow waited by St. Valentine's Fountain, but Boy did not come. As the night deepened, the temperature fell from freezing to well below that. For a while she stood and chatted to an old woman huddled over a brazier of roasting chestnuts, until finally the cold was too much. Though Willow had said nothing, the old woman glanced back at her.

"He ain't coming, you know," she said, and before Willow could reply, shuffled away.

Willow started to worry. They were supposed to have met as the church bells rang seven, but it was long after nine by now. Willow had studied every inch of the frozen fountain, whose long icicles hung from its spout like tusks, where in the summer the water gushed.

Something must have happened to Boy. She thought about what the old woman had said. Something must have happened to him, because there could be no mistaking the plans they had made.

Unless . . . what if she had misread him? She had been doing most of the talking; maybe she had just heard what she wanted to hear, that Boy wanted to come with her.

She stamped around on the snowy ground by the fountain, getting colder all the time.

It had all seemed so easy sitting in the Feather the night before, but out in the freezing streets it was different. How would they find somewhere to live? She wasn't earning enough to feed them both, let alone rent a room. Perhaps Boy had thought it over; perhaps he'd realized how stupid it was, and maybe he didn't even want her the way she wanted him. He was living in splendor now, relatively. Kepler had given him clothes and a proper room with a real bed in a well-to-do house. It even had that amazing system of electrical lighting Kepler had created. Why on earth would Boy want to leave all that to come and live on the streets again?

She hadn't even known Boy that well at the theater. It was only in those last five days of the year, when she and Boy had become entwined in Valerian's terrible adventure, that she had realized that she felt something for him.

Willow brushed some snow off the edge of the fountain's basin and sat down. She put her head in her hands and cried.

The bell of St. Valentine's Church chimed ten.

Now Willow was angry. If Boy had decided not to be with her, the least he could have done was tell her to her face, rather than leave her freezing by the fountain. Her anger grew as she began to feel shamed: how foolish she was to believe Boy cared about her.

She'd let him know how angry she was!

She set off for Kepler's house. She'd been there only twice, briefly, but she knew she could find the way. It would be a long walk, but then, at least she would be moving, and might feel a little warmer.

She was in a fury, and as she walked as fast as she was able along the snowbound alleys of the City, her mood did not improve. But now as she turned into the Square of Adam and Sophia, something softened in her. Though her route did not take her that way, she knew she was only a street or two away from the Reach, where she and Boy had been together just over a week before. It was enough to trigger a flood of memories of the fraught time they had spent trying to save Valerian's life, only to have him try to take Boy's in return. Maybe they had been wrong about Valerian, but she couldn't be wrong about Boy; there was no way to fake what had passed between them, and she began to worry again. Something must have happened to him.

When she got to Kepler's front door, it flew open almost the moment she pulled the bell handle.

"Oh, it's you. Where is he?"

Kepler seemed distracted, even a little angry, but Willow could see that he too was worried.

"Where is he?" Kepler asked again.

"Can I come in?" Willow said. "Please. I'm freezing."

Kepler blinked.

"Yes . . . ," he said, standing aside.

He pushed the door closed behind her and ushered her into the study.

"Well?" Kepler asked, as Willow moved to stand in front of the fire. "Have you seen him?"

Willow shook her head. She suddenly felt incredibly numb. Her teeth chattered and she started to shake.

Kepler pulled a chair up by the fireplace for her, muttering as he did so. He fished around in his desk, and pulled out a small bottle that Willow recognized.

It was the drug that Valerian had taken so much of in the days before he died. She shook her head, afraid of what it might do to her, but Kepler ignored her protests.

He poured a capful of the green liquid into her mouth, and waited. Warmth and strength began to wash over Willow in a delightful way, and she immediately felt herself begin to recover. She felt light-headed, even felt like laughing.

Kepler pulled another chair up by the fire and sat down.

"Well, Willow?" he asked again.

Willow shook her head. "I came here to find him. We were supposed to meet. . . ."

She stopped, realizing she shouldn't have told Kepler that, but he seemed too preoccupied to notice or to care, staring down into the fire.

"I sent him out earlier, he was supposed to come straight back. . . ."

"Where?" asked Willow.

Kepler looked up at her.

"What?"

"Where did you send him?"

"To Valerian's."

"You sent him there!" cried Willow. "You shouldn't have sent him there, anything might have—"

"What?" Kepler snapped. "What might have happened to him? It's an empty house. There's nothing dangerous there. Not now. Not now Valerian's gone."

"You still shouldn't have made him go there. . . . It's a bad place for him."

Kepler shrugged. "I don't want him hurt any more than you do."

"Really?" said Willow sharply. "Why is that?"

"I assure you I want the best for him. You could not understand."

"Well, if you did you wouldn't have sent him there."

Kepler opened his mouth to bite back at Willow, but then shut it again. He thought briefly, frowning. "What matters is this. Where is he? There's nowhere else for him to go, except back on the streets, and this is the coldest winter in memory."

Willow nodded.

"You're right. I'm sorry. I'm just worried that . . ."

"The Yellow House. That's the only place to look. You can stay here and get warm, I'll be—"

"No," Willow said firmly, getting to her feet. "I'm coming too."

"Nonsense," said Kepler. "You aren't fit to go anywhere. I look after the boy now. You can stay here until—"

"No!" shouted Willow. "I'm coming with you. You have no right to tell me what to do. If you care anything for how I feel, then you'll give me another drink of that stuff and help me find Boy!"

With that Kepler thrust the bottle at Willow and went off to find a coat.

Willow smiled as he went, took another sip of the drug and put the bottle in her pocket. She found Kepler in the hall, wrestling with a long winter coat. By his feet was a canvas shoulder pack, which he picked up and swung onto his back.

"Well?" he said.

"Let's go, Mr. Kepler," Willow said brightly, and led the way to the door and out into the snow-swirling night.

The Dungeon

The Place of Deceitful Histories

✤

1

Boy's first view of the Imperial Palace of Emperor Frederick III was not welcoming.

The cart trundled wearily uphill toward the palace walls for ages, but when almost at the gates, turned onto a path that wound back down around the outskirts of the mound on which the walls were built. This path reached an end at a solid iron gate right at the base of the palace hill. Behind it a long, low tunnel led deep into the earth under the palace buildings.

Boy looked up at the moldy ceiling of the tunnel as the cart was manhandled along it by torchlight, being too small for the horse to make it down. Every now and again the tunnel was pitted by defensive openings, through which arrows or crossbow bolts could be fired should anyone try to attack the palace by this particular route.

Far above Boy's head, through the bedrock of the palace hill, perched the magnificent, sprawling splendor of the palace itself, but Boy saw nothing of this. Up in the dark night sky, the palace burned like a precious jewel, torches and lights flaring from every ornate window, picking out a gleam here and there from the gilded dome of the palace chapel, or the spire of the bell tower. The palace was a place of wonder, made to impress the onlooker with the greatness of the imperial line, and to dwarf the ordinary mortal. It had been built over many years, each emperor adding something new, trying to find a way of outdoing his predecessor, with a more elaborate spire, or a more preposterous tower. The result was a vast, heaven-reaching concoction of architectural hallucination, all teetering on a low hill south of the river. The palace faced in on itself; the wonder was not, after all, for the rabble in the City to admire. They were impressed enough by the high walls and battlements that marked its perimeter. The true splendor of the place was only visible from inside; from the Great Court or the Emperor's Green or the Royal Gardens. Then one could stop and stand and stare openmouthed at the acres of gilded rooftops, copper-topped cupolas and sculpted marble embellishments.

Much of its finery was presently hidden under several feet of snow, but Boy saw none of it anyway. He was shuffled down the tunnel into a wider, higher space deep underground, where the cart was upended and he, along with all Valerian's other possessions, fell out onto the cold, unforgiving flagstones.

He heard the squeak of a door or gates, and then the sound of a heavy lock being secured. Footsteps led away, and then all was quiet.

Boy tried to wriggle onto his backside, and having achieved this, managed to sit up and lean against the wall.

All around was blackness. His wrist still hurt from the fall in the house, and he was cold and tired.

Straining to see anything at all, he suddenly became aware of something.

A noise.

It was faint at first, then got a little louder, coming nearer to him. The sound was a shuffling, a scraping, soft but heavy, and with it there seemed to be a low, rasping breathing, like a creature half throttled. But almost as soon as Boy was convinced it was not mere imagination, the sound receded and then disappeared entirely, leaving something else behind. A smell.

The smell of fresh blood.

2

Willow and Kepler stood on the doorstep of the Yellow House, and knew something was wrong. Neither of them had a key to the house, but they didn't need one. The snow on the porch and outside the house was a confused mess of footsteps and the tracks of cartwheels. The door was ajar.

"Thieves?" whispered Kepler.

"They could still be in there," Willow said, her voice wavering.

"Then we'd better tread quietly."

Kepler took a step forward, and as he did, his foot kicked something lying in the snow. He looked down and picked it up. With surprise he saw it was the lens.

"What is it?" Willow asked.

"It's the very thing I sent Boy here to collect."

They both fell silent, and looked again at the open door of the Yellow House.

It was dark in the house and they had brought no light.

As they made their way gingerly inside, Willow and Kepler waited for their eyes to grow accustomed to the gloom. Only the faintest shimmer of light made its way into the house from the torchlit street, showing feebly through the grimy windows high up in the hall.

They listened keenly, but though no sound could be heard, they didn't relax. The house seemed predatory, like a vicious animal waiting to pounce.

They moved upstairs and found themselves drawn inexorably to the spiral staircase that led to the Tower.

There was a little more light drifting down through the high glass skylight above the third-floor landing, and they were able to pick their way up to the Tower more easily, but still they went cautiously.

Instinctively, they had found their way to the wounded heart of the house. Kepler led the way, and they immediately saw that the Tower room had had its guts ripped out. The room was stripped of almost everything valuable. All the books were gone, all the scientific apparatus and magical paraphernalia that had given it its identity. All that was left was anything that was too big to move or was broken, the projection table of the camera obscura and the old leather armchair.

Kepler shook his head.

"What in God's name has happened here?" he said.

Willow said nothing.

"Dare we risk some light?" she asked. "He kept a packet of matches on the windowsill. . . ."

Willow fumbled in the gloom, but soon she found the matches where she had seen them last.

Kepler turned to her and nodded.

"Very well," he said. "The villains are long gone."

Willow struck a match, and held it up above her head, letting its feeble light cast a glow around the room.

"Look out!" she shouted suddenly, but at the same moment Kepler had seen that the trapdoor lay wide open, the hatch a gaping black mouth in the floor just inches from where he stood.

He stepped back a pace.

"So they stole everything they could. . . ."

"Who?"

Kepler shrugged.

"I don't know."

"But where's Boy?" Willow asked.

Kepler looked around the mess.

Willow squealed and dropped the match, which had burned to her fingertips.

"Quick!" Kepler said. "Light another one! I saw something."

Willow struck another match and once more a little patch of light spread around them.

"There!" said Kepler. "Over there!"

"What is it?" Willow asked, and followed Kepler carefully to the edge of the hole left by the trapdoor, where something on the floor had caught his eye.

He picked it up.

It was a white feather.

"What?" asked Willow, desperately. "What does it mean?"

"It means that our crooks were rather powerful people. And I think it means I know where Boy is. The Imperial Palace."

"How do you know?" Willow asked.

"The feather. The feather is from the uniform of an Imperial Guardsman. That's where he is."

Willow dropped the match, and they were left in darkness again.

"I will get him out," Kepler said, but not really to Willow.

"I'll help. I'll come too."

"Not this time, girl!" Kepler declared. "I've had enough of you tailing around. Boy is mine, and I don't need your help with anything. Not least Boy. You go back to the orphanage and be grateful I found you a job!"

Willow said nothing.

She knew what she was going to do whether Kepler liked it or not, and there was no point in arguing about it. Without another word she left the Tower, and the house, behind her.

Kepler stood in the ruins of the Tower, brooding.

"Boy!" he said to the thick dark air. "This wasn't supposed to happen. Not yet. But your fate is mine now. You will be mine."

He pulled the lens from his pocket and held it tight in his fist.

"And I have this, at least. . . ."

3

For a long, long time Boy saw nothing, heard nothing. It was as if he had become deaf and blind, and panic began to well up inside him. Finally he could stand no more, and as much to prove he had not gone deaf as anything else, he shouted into the darkness.

"Hello! Hello?"

His voice fell dead around him, with a short, curtailed echo. It reminded him of those dank underground tunnels where he had been pursued by Valerian, and he didn't like the memory one bit.

"Please! Please don't leave me here!"

The heavy silence covered him the moment his voice was killed by the close stone walls and low damp ceiling. He was about to cry out for a third time, when he caught a whiff of the smell he had sensed before. His heart beat faster, but he heard nothing. Maybe it wasn't such a good idea to be calling out into the nothingness.

He put his head back on the cold stone floor, and still trussed up like a slaughtered beast, he lay motionless for a while.

*   *   *

He must have slept.

He was woken up by being pulled roughly by his ankles from where he lay.

Hands seemed to be everywhere, grabbing him, but he still couldn't see anything, dazzled by the light from several oil lamps.

"What . . . ?" he tried to say, but was winded as he was thrown over someone's shoulder.

"Get on with it," said a voice. "He's in a foul mood. And he wants it all now."

"As usual," said another voice.

In an instant Boy was swung away down a low, gloomy tunnel, but he felt that they were rising this time, headed up to the real world. He was glad of that, at least. Maybe there would be someone he could talk to, to explain things and get himself set free. It all had to be a silly mistake; he couldn't *really* belong to the emperor. Like most people in the City, Boy knew little of the emperor, just vague stories about him, that he was very old, and maybe a little crazy. No one knew anything for sure.

As his eyes grew used to the lights bobbing ahead of him, he saw that he was being carried by one of a long line of men, each with some burden or other. He was hanging upside down, and it was hard to be sure, but as the file of carriers made its way into a larger and this time torchlit tunnel, he saw what it was they were carrying. Valerian's things. All of them.

Before he had time to wonder what was going on, Boy sensed something else. That smell again. He twisted around to see its source, and in the dim light could just make out a small, rough-cut entrance to a flight of stairs leading down from the corridor they were in. It was barred by an iron grille, with a padlocked chain holding it shut.

Beyond the grille, Boy could see that the stairs were narrow, and hideously steep. It made him feel sick merely looking at them. They plunged down into darkness and there was no sign that they ever ended.

"Stop wriggling, you monkey," snarled the man carrying Boy. He let himself hang loosely again and they moved past the entrance to the dark flight down.

They were still trudging upward, and now turned and climbed three stone steps. Then there was a doorway, and suddenly the light was brilliant all around them.

They were in a long and ornate corridor, with a polished wooden floor. Bright morning daylight poured in through tall leaded windows. Along the walls hung huge, elaborately framed portraits of people in royal attire.

The corridor seemed to stretch forever, and when they finally left it, they turned and the long file of men made their way down another identical gallery.

As they went, taking a flight of stairs here, and entering and leaving countless golden-glimmering rooms and passages, Boy finally understood that he really was in the Imperial Palace.

He heard voices ahead, and saw from his upside-down point of view that they were in a chamber large enough to be a ballroom. Huge windows took up much of one wall, flooding the room with more light than Boy's eyes could bear for the time being. He squinted as he was dumped onto a tabletop, blinking and trying to get the right way up.

"Stay there, you little brat!" snapped his porter, and cuffed him round the head. Boy lay, blinking.

As he got used to the light he gradually opened his eyes a little more, and dared to look around. Men were standing in groups; others were still filing in from where Boy had come, all bearing more and more of Valerian's things. Boy lost count of how many came in carrying a stack of a dozen or so thick leather-bound books, depositing their burdens on long polished oak tables, just like the one he was lying on.

Occasionally someone would glance at him, but when he tried to get their attention, they ignored him, merely regarding him as if he was an animal, or some curiosity in a marketplace.

Suddenly there was a commotion, and the porters hurried frantically along the tables and made their way out. A trumpet blast sounded at the far end of the hall, and the groups broke up to form an orderly line. They all bowed, ridiculously low.

A nervous voice cried out.

"His Imperial Majesty, His Royal Greatness, Emperor Frederick!"

Boy twisted round where he lay and regarded the far end of the room.

A tall, imposing figure in flowing bloodred robes swept into the room. The silence was total.

Boy, like many people in the City itself, had often doubted that there was an emperor at all behind the high walls of the palace. No one had seen him in years, life in the City seemed to go on perfectly well by itself, and some people even believed him to be nothing more than a legend.

Now, right before his eyes, Boy saw an impressive, powerful man with a shaven head striding down the length of the ballroom, and knew the rumors were false. Another figure trailed after the first. A small old man, richly dressed but shrunken, hobbled in after the emperor, who stood waiting with his hand resting on a high-backed chair, so sumptuous it could have been a throne.

Boy watched, puzzled. The line of men still bowed with their noses near their knees, while the old man scurried along, taking short hopping steps. He reached the throne, and sat down in it, then put his head back, his eyes closed.

Finally he opened them again, and turned to look at the tall man beside him.

"This had better be worth it, Maxim," he whined. "I haven't been down to the Eastern State Rooms since . . . well, I can't remember, but there's far too many flights of stairs on the way. You should have had a chair sent for me."

"My apologies, Emperor," said Maxim.

And now Boy understood. The decrepit little man was the emperor, not the tall figure in red.

Emperor Frederick. The last of his line, at least eighty years old, with no kin to succeed him.

"I do indeed believe," Maxim went on, "that you should see everything we recovered from the magician's house. And I recall that you did yourself say that the Eastern Ballroom would be the only place large enough—"

"Nonsense!" snapped Frederick. "I said no such thing. I never change my mind, you know that! What's wrong with the court? That's twice the size, and several floors closer to my chambers! Dare you contradict me, Maxim?"

"Indeed no," said Maxim, flatly. "I do not question you,

74

sire. But some of the items were . . . a trifle awkward to carry that far. Shall we?"

Maxim gestured for Frederick to join him, but the emperor shut his eyes and shook his head.

"I can see from here. You may begin."

Maxim clicked his fingers. The line of bowing courtiers jerked upright, some a little faster than others. One or two older ones straightened very slowly, a hand clasped to the small of their backs. They made their way over to join Maxim, who was walking along the line of tables, inspecting the things lying there.

Unable to move himself upright, Boy had a rather sideways view of what was going on. Nonetheless, he could sense there was something familiar about Maxim. It was in the way he moved, the way he looked at the emperor and the way he seemed to be restraining his voice whenever he spoke. There was something restless about him, something hungry, though Boy did not know what it was exactly.

"Magical apparatus, sire!" Maxim announced from across the room.

Frederick yawned, opened his eyes for a second, then shut them again.

"Why did we have to do this so early in the day?" he sniped at Maxim. "You know my stomach hurts if I have to arise early."

"It's nearly noon," Maxim said, calmly, "and I thought the matter too urgent to wait. This magical equipment could hold the secret to occult powers that may aid us in our quest."

Boy looked at the things Maxim had indicated and frowned. He didn't see that a box that chickens disappeared

75

into, and a device for making smoke screens for Valerian's stage act were going to be of much use for anything the emperor could be interested in.

Maxim and the other members of court moved on, then stopped at the next group of tables.

"Books, sire," Maxim announced to Frederick, who remained with his eyes shut, and waved a hand dismissively.

"What of it? We have lots of books."

Maxim bit his tongue.

"Yes, sire, but the magician was known to have certain books of considerable power. Certain. Books."

He paused, thinking Frederick would respond to this, but the Emperor was barely listening. Maxim sighed and went on.

"It may be that some answer to our search lies within one of these tomes. I will bend my researches in their direction, scour every page for the slightest clue."

He flourished a hand at the hundreds of books stacked in crazy piles on the tables.

And that should keep him off my back for a while, Maxim thought, but said nothing. Instead, he spread a large and very fake smile across his face and continued.

"In fact," Maxim went on, "I am convinced our solution lies in that direction. The magician . . ."

But Maxim stopped midsentence. He had seen something that surprised him. Curled up on one of the tables, with hands and legs tied behind him, was a thin youth with spiky hair.

For a moment Maxim was thrown. He glanced at one of the porters, who rapidly whispered in his ear.

"The magician's famulus!" Maxim declared.

Frederick coughed and opened his eyes. He followed Maxim's hand pointing to where Boy lay.

"His what?" he spluttered.

"His assistant," Maxim replied. "His apprentice. His . . . boy. We found him in the ruins of the house, he belonged to the magician. We believe he may be of considerable use in explaining many of the practices and skills of the magician himself."

Boy frowned, wishing he could scratch an itch that had started on his nose.

There was silence. The emperor stared, his little eyes blinking slowly.

"Maxim, I have had enough," he said.

"But, sire, this is a great development in our search. We are getting closer—"

"Shut up!" Frederick whined. "Shut up! We are not getting closer to anything. I am getting closer to lunchtime, and I haven't even had my breakfast yet."

"Sire . . ."

"And you, Maxim, are getting closer to the executioner's block."

"Sire, I—"

"Understand me, Maxim. I mean you to succeed in this quest. That is vital. But *how* you do it is of no interest to me whatsoever. Understand? So get me a chair to take me to breakfast, and make sure that damn chef does the eggs properly. You know they make me ill if they're too runny. I swear he's trying to kill me."

"Yes, sire, I—" Maxim tried again, but the emperor was not listening.

"I'm running out of patience, really I am. You had better

find an answer soon. Where's that blasted chair? I can't wait all day, you know. I won't have time for breakfast before lunch and you know that I get a headache if I don't get enough rest between meals. You're trying to kill me too! Well, I won't have it."

The emperor got to his feet.

"Come, Maxim! We shall walk back, though you know how my feet ache. If I faint on the way you'll have to carry me."

He scurried away down the hall, and Maxim followed.

"Keep up, Maxim, keep up," Frederick was saying. "Oh, and one more thing. Have that brat thrown into the river. He's dirty and probably spreading disease. You have no thought for my welfare! None at all! He's only some street brat on the make, you know. Honestly! There's thousands of them just like him out there! This whole city is like a scabrous beggar holding out its hands for a penny. Well, I won't have it. Throw him in the river and then get me my breakfast. Maxim!"

He had reached the end of the hall and disappeared round a corner.

"Sire," Maxim called, hurrying after him. "Coming, sire."

Boy had jolted upright. He tried to sit up and in doing so fell off his table.

Guards hurried over to where he lay writhing on the floor.

"Right," said one of the courtiers, "you heard His Majesty. In the river with him."

With that, several hands clutched at Boy's clothes. Once again he was thrown over someone's shoulder.

"No!" he cried. "No!"

As he made to scream again, a rolled-up handkerchief was shoved into his mouth.

"Get on with it," someone said. "We've got enough to do today as it is."

4

Boy struggled, but four pairs of hands held him firmly, so firmly that there was no chance of escape.

He spat the handkerchief from his mouth.

"You can't do this!" he yelled as he tried to kick out at the men carrying him. "I've done nothing! You can't do this!"

The men did not reply, but one of them struck Boy across the back of his head with an open hand.

"Little brat!" he said, to his companions.

They were hurrying down a narrow dark passage, the rough-cut stone floor sloping away before them.

"Would be easier just to chuck him down there," one of them muttered.

"Where?"

"You know where I mean."

"And save some other poor soul," said another voice.

"You heard what he said," said the second voice. "Put him in the river and get back to work."

There was no more talk after that.

The men renewed their pace; Boy doubled his efforts to break free and was cuffed around the head again, and punched in the ribs this time too. Now he heard the sound of water rushing past somewhere nearby.

"Right, then, let's be done with it."

Boy knew they were standing by an underground quay. He could hear and smell the running water, and knew he was once more at the edge of the subterranean water-world of canals and catacombs through which he had been relentlessly pursued by Valerian in the Dead Days before the end of the year. So there was at least one connection from the palace to that cold, damp hidden city beneath the City itself.

"Right!" shouted one of the men. "On three . . ."

Boy had given up trying to plead, but tried to wriggle and kick harder than ever. He was helpless, and he knew that as soon as he hit the water he would sink like a stone.

"One!" the man shouted.

"Two!"

There was another shout from behind them.

"Hold!"

Boy already recognized that commanding voice: Maxim.

Two of the men hesitated. The third had already begun to swing Boy's knees out, and lost his grip. Boy's bottom half sank under the water. The two holding him by the shoulders nearly overbalanced and followed him into the water.

Maxim ran over to the men. With his help, Boy was easily retrieved from the under-river.

The men stood back from where Boy now lay on the quayside.

"Sire?" one of them said, looking up at Maxim.

81

Boy could sense the basis of the relationship between the men and Maxim. It was something he knew well from life with Valerian: fear.

Valerian. Boy now knew who Maxim had reminded him of when he had first seen him in the ballroom. They shared the same strange mix of desperation and frightening power.

Maxim surveyed the scene before him. He wrung the sleeve of his robe, which had dipped into the water.

"The emperor may not think he needs the boy," he said, "but I do. Leave him with me."

The men shuffled away a step or two, heading back for the steps to the palace.

"Very good, sire," said one.

Boy rolled over and managed to get to his knees. He looked up at Maxim.

"Oh," Maxim said, as they went. "One more thing. Forget what happened here. If anyone asks, you threw the boy in the river as you were told. I'll see to him from now."

Boy, soaked from the waist down, dripped onto the stone flags and shivered, finding no comfort at all in Maxim's words.

5

Boy's body lay asleep one hundred and fifty feet below the shiny bright marble floor of the court, but his mind was elsewhere. In feverish dreaming he made his way along a stone corridor, crumbling and night black. He thought he would stop at the top of the flight of stone steps he had been expecting, but with alarm found that he had already begun to go down them, step by steep step.

Unable to stop, his feet moved by themselves, drawing him deeper down toward the thing waiting for him. For he knew without question that something lived at the foot of the dark flight of stairs, something that could take his life from him.

The stairs were narrow, their treads not even wide enough for him to get the whole of his foot on each one, and they were so sickeningly steep as to make his head reel.

He looked round and could no longer see the entrance at the top of the stairs. Panicking, he turned and missed his footing. He slipped forward, tipping headlong down the awful staircase, plummeting toward the thing.

He screamed.

He woke.

6

Boy had no idea how long he'd been in the cell.

After Maxim had saved him from being drowned in the under-river, he'd been dragged by his neck down unfathomable passages to a high-vaulted chamber somewhere deep beneath the palace. Around its walls were a series of cells, constructed from iron bars on three sides, and whose backs were the stone wall of the dungeon itself. The bars ran right up to the roof, so there was no way to climb over them.

Boy could see at least three cells on either side of him, and a similar row on the far side of the chamber, which was lit by a smoky oil lamp hanging on a vast chain that dangled from the center of the ceiling.

Maxim had swung the door of his cell shut and clanked a key in its lock.

"I'll be back" was all he had said, and he left.

Boy had not been searched by any of his captors, and still had his lockpick in his pocket.

Having waited a good while after Maxim had left, Boy looked about him. As far as he could see in the half-light, there was no one in any of the other cells, but once or twice he wondered if he had heard something on the other side of the room.

He rummaged around in the lock and soon flicked the tumblers into their right positions. The lock turned and Boy once more paused and looked about. Still nothing. He tiptoed out of his cell, and moved to the center of the chamber, underneath the oil lamp.

In the darkness, Boy could not see all of the dungeon at once. He could just make out groups of cells against the walls, and in the space in the middle he saw a simple fireplace with a stand for a pot or cauldron to be hung above it. In the middle of the room there was also a table of sorts, and a chair, more like a wooden throne. Boy went closer. The table and chair reminded him for a moment of some of the bits of equipment Valerian had used in their stage act, but then he realized what they were. A chair with locks on the arms, a table with a ratchet at the end.

Boy decided not to wait any longer.

The floor of the dungeon sloped slightly up at one side, and in the wall on the highest side was the door through which Maxim had left.

Boy made for the door quickly, and tried the handle. It was locked, of course, and there was no keyhole on the inside.

Boy's heart began to pound, and he shook the handle violently. It was no use. He sat down on the floor with his back to the door, trying to decide what to do.

He sat still, thinking about how he might escape at first, but as he failed to find any solution other thoughts came to mind. He thought of Willow, of where she was and what she was doing. He wondered what she might be thinking after he had not turned up by the fountain.

His brooding was interrupted by the sound of footsteps. He got up and as quickly as he could skipped back to his cell, locking the door behind him. If he was going to be stuck, then he reasoned it was a good idea not to let his captors know he could pick locks, and that he could at least get out of the inner cell. Just as Boy hid the lockpick in his pocket once more, the far door banged open.

Boy was surprised and also somewhat relieved to see that it was not Maxim who entered the room, but a small, crooked man, bald, in shabby clothes. That at least meant that one other person knew where Boy was, that his life was not solely dependent on Maxim's interests in him.

The man carried a tray on which were two bowls. He came over to Boy's cell, and put the tray on the floor. Only now could Boy see that the man was blind. His eyes were open but stared blankly, focusing on nothing. Boy wondered how he was able to move across the chamber to the one cell where Boy was without hesitating. It must mean he had done it many, many times before.

The blind jailer picked one of the bowls up and slid it between the bars.

"There you go," he said. "Make it last."

Boy looked in the wooden bowl and saw a slop of gray sludge. There was no spoon.

The man got to his feet and picked up the tray once more, taking the other bowl with it.

"Wait!" Boy cried. "Don't go! Tell me what's going on! What are they going to do with me?"

The man didn't stop.

"I've no idea," he said as he went. "I just bring the food."

"Wait! Please come back!" Boy called, but the jailer was already away on the far side of the chamber, and paid Boy no more attention.

He got up, and paced around the cell, trying not to think about anything other than how to get out of the foul hole in which he found himself.

After a while he stopped, having failed to come up with anything, though it occurred to him that there was something significant he had learnt.

He had learnt that there was someone in one of the other cells—the second bowl of food must have been for another prisoner.

Boy looked at his own food.

He determined to eat it, then go to find out who else was locked up in the dungeon, but he had taken no more than a mouthful before the oil lamp began to flicker and die.

Very soon it gave up the ghost entirely, and Boy finished his food in darkness. Unable to see, he dared not venture out, and lay down.

Some time later, he heard, or at least thought he heard, a sound. The sound of someone singing. It was so faint that he couldn't be sure he wasn't imagining it, and very soon he could hear nothing more at all, though he strained to do so.

Since then he had heard nothing else, nor seen anything else. With no stimulus to his senses, all that lay before his eyes was a ghost image—the image of a stone staircase dropping down to the dark unknown.

7

For two days Willow had hung around near the palace walls, trying to find some way into the vast complex of buildings. Despite its size, the palace had relatively few entrances, to make its defense easier. In fact the palace had never been attacked by any invading force or local uprising. Long before, when the power of the empire still existed, its strength had been so great that no army would have ever dared to invade. These days, the empire was long gone, the palace was a strange curiosity to most people, and though it still governed the City in name, most decisions were taken by various guilds, leagues and organizations. The City and the palace largely ignored each other.

Still, due to the paranoia and vanity of a succession of peculiar emperors, each dottier than the last, the palace retained notions that it was a castle, and as a result, ingress to and egress from it were strictly controlled. Despite its current state of decline, the reputation of the palace as a seat of influence, wealth and great learning remained alluring to travelers across the entire continent.

Willow had run away from the orphanage without even collecting a week's pay. For the first time in her life she was out on the streets, and had already started to learn what it must have been like for Boy all those years. Hunger had taken the edge off her sharp sense of right and wrong, and she had stolen some bread from a street merchant. As soon as she had eaten it, however, she felt guilty, and vowed she would pay the man back three times over when she could.

Now she sat on a stone bollard across the street from one of the main entrances to the palace, the East Gate. Like the only other main entrance, the North Gate, this way into the palace was heavily guarded, and fortified. Willow had watched for hours to see if there was some chink in the armor that might offer her a chance to get inside, but she had seen none. Every trader or visitor had to present themselves at a grilled window, and explain the purpose of their visit. Many of them seemed to wave a paper document or similar at the guard inside before the heavy iron spiked portcullis was raised to allow them in.

There was no way in through the East Gate unless you had official business. It was exactly the same at the North Gate, Willow knew, because she had spent several hours there the day before doing just the same thing.

She sat disconsolately on her bollard, getting colder by the minute. It was late afternoon, and the snow fell incessantly. It had been days since anyone had seen the sun, and the City was grinding to a halt. Willow had heard two merchants muttering that there would be food shortages soon if the snow went on. They seemed solemn for a moment, then laughed about putting their prices up as supplies became scarcer.

Willow got up and began to walk around the palace

again. There was a cobbled street that ran right around its base. It was called the Planting, because on either side the street was lined with lime trees. In the summer they provided beautiful rustling shade from the sun; in the winter they were bare, stripped things that pointed fingers rudely at the sky.

Willow had walked nearly a mile and was close to the North Gate once more. As she gazed at its impenetrable face yet again, she noticed something.

Keeping herself alert to all the comings and goings, she watched one particular man. He was carrying a large bag on his shoulders, and after a lengthy conversation with two of the guards, was let in through the outer gates.

Willow ran forward, and was in time to see the man being escorted by another guard up the sloping road that led to the inner gates.

Suddenly she heard footsteps close in behind her, and before she could turn felt her arms grabbed from behind.

She wrenched herself free and spun around.

"You!" she cried.

In front of her stood Kepler, scowling.

"Willow," he said. "Why am I not surprised to see you here?"

8

On the third day Maxim paid Boy a visit.

He stood outside the cell in which Boy had been moldering, by turns sleeping and waking, ravaged by hunger.

"You, boy," he said. "What's your name?"

Boy wondered what he meant. Maxim stared at him, fixing him to the spot. Boy looked back at him. He was tall, perhaps as tall as Valerian, but he was bigger, heavier. His face was somewhat round, giving way to the passing years maybe, but it was nevertheless striking, with strong eyes and nose. He had no hair, which made his large ears even more pronounced. He had the devil's own deep voice.

"Answer me, you insolent boy!" he barked at Boy. "What is your name?"

Now Boy understood. Of course, the man in front of him didn't know he was called Boy.

"Boy," Boy said.

"Don't try to be clever with me," Maxim threatened, "or my patience may run out quicker than you would like."

"I'm not. Boy's my name."

Maxim paused.

"You . . ."

"I don't have a name," Boy said helpfully.

"You must have a name," Maxim said. "What do people call you?"

"Boy. They call me Boy. That's what I'm trying to tell you. I grew up on the streets. No one knows who my parents are."

"How touching," said Maxim unkindly. "Very well. I shall call you Boy too. Listen to me, Boy. You are going to help me. I need information. And you're going to give it to me. If you tell me what I need to know, I will reward you by letting you go free from here. Back to the streets. If you fail me, you'll die down here."

Boy took a step back, despite the bars between them.

"What . . . ," he said, "what you want me to do? I don't know anything."

"Yes, you do. Yes," Maxim said. "You were until recently the famulus of the magician, Valerian. Correct?"

Boy did not answer.

"Correct?" Maxim shouted.

"Yes," said Boy. "Yes, I was."

"Then you must have been privy to his dealings. I know you assisted him in his work, both on- and offstage. Don't look surprised. You think I don't have men out in the City? I have spies everywhere and I know much about Valerian. For example, I know he was more than just a stage conjuror. Correct?"

Boy nodded.

"Yes, but I never really knew—"

"Be quiet, Boy," Maxim said harshly. "Wait until I ask you to think. Now, I know you know about his magical skills, and I also know he was looking for something shortly before his death. A book. You know about that?"

Boy went cold.

"No," he said. "I don't know about any book."

Maxim stepped right up to the bars of the cell.

"You're lying. Don't lie to me, Boy, or I will get someone down here to hurt you. Tell me about the book."

Just to hear mention of the book was enough to put a chill in Boy's heart. He had seen what it had done to Valerian and Kepler, he knew of its deceitful power. And yet he wanted it too.

"I don't know what you mean," said Boy, backing away across the cell. His heels suddenly hit the back wall and he jumped. "I mean," he said, "I know a little about his tricks, and I know he had lots of books, but I don't know anything about them. I can't read very well, you see."

"Be quiet!" Maxim said. "Don't play games with me! I know you know about one particular book, one very special book. Where is it? Did Valerian find it before he died? Tell me!"

Boy shook his head, and hoped his voice wasn't shaking too badly.

"I don't know," he cried, "I really don't. I know about his tricks and some of the equipment, but I don't know about a special book."

Maxim turned away, scowling. Boy held his breath, wondering if he'd been convincing enough. His mind was racing, as he frantically tried to work out whether Maxim could know about the book, and if so, from whom. And, more crucially, what he wanted it for.

Maxim turned back to him.

"That's enough for now," he said. He gave no sign betraying whether he believed Boy's story. "I'll be back soon. And you will be more forthcoming next time. I promise you that. I have plenty of need for blood down here, Boy, so think about what you do, and don't, know. Think very carefully."

He moved off, still glowering at Boy, and then turned on his heel and spun away through the door.

9

Maxim chewed his lip. He waited, at the right hand of Frederick's throne, while the emperor considered the situation before him.

The court was full. The usual crowd was there.

The doctors. A feckless assortment with less knowledge of medicine than Maxim, but they served their purpose. Frederick was never well. At least, in his mind there was always something wrong with him. The doctors were very useful to Maxim. He could, and did, blame them for the emperor's poor state of health, deflecting from himself any complaints Frederick made. And if, as rarely happened, Frederick chanced to say he felt a bit better than usual one morning, Maxim would take the praise, pretending he had told the doctors to improve their efforts.

There were the stargazers, the astrologists. Maxim had less control of this group. Not that they were any less spineless than the doctors, but they were altogether unpredictable. They wore the badges of their office—pointed caps emblazoned with stars—and carried charts and diagrams with them always. Frederick set great store by astrological computations, and never did anything if Saturn was in retrograde motion. Maxim did his best to use the information the astrologers imparted to further his own position, but they were apt to come out with the most unexpected bit of news at any time, with little or no warning, and Frederick would be sent into fits of panic. When this happened he was likely to start accusing Maxim of disloyalty, or even treason, and at the very least criticized Maxim's lack of care for his emperor, and his emperor's health and general well-being.

There were alchemists, necromancers and other magical practitioners whom Frederick had seen fit to assemble around him. Many of them were entirely laughable and ineffectual, but some were devious and clever enough to give Maxim cause for concern. Frederick seemed to think the answer to his problems lay with men of this sort. He never welcomed Maxim's suggestions that there were perhaps too many of them and that he might do better with a dozen fewer.

Then there was the court itself, with its entourages and hangers-on, the noblemen and ladies of the court, all from rich and powerful families, dukes and duchesses, lords and ladies, but not one with a direct claim to the throne. This was the group Maxim feared the most in the event of Frederick's death. They were a conniving and greedy bunch out for nothing but their own gain. Maxim recognized these motives well, since they were his own, and to be feared in others.

Then there were the staff, though most of them existed almost unseen.

It was Maxim's lot to rule this exotic collection, to see that things in the palace ran smoothly, to make sure

Frederick was attended to in the smallest detail, every minute of every day.

Now Maxim stood by Frederick's throne as the emperor considered the application of another occultist.

The influence of Frederick's court was not what it had once been, but stories of its very real wealth still spread far and wide, and it was commonplace for several new applicants to arrive at the palace gates each week, all hoping to gain the special favor of the emperor and earn a fortune in the process.

This latest candidate was a youngish man, with thin hair and roaming eyes. Maxim, however, was fretting not about him, but about the boy in the dungeon. Maxim was convinced that Boy had to know about the book. His spies had told him that it had been rediscovered, and Maxim knew that Valerian had been looking for it. If he *had* found it, then it stood to reason that his boy had to know its current whereabouts.

Maxim now quite rightly believed the book would be the only way to find a solution to his predicament. There had to be some way out of the dilemma Frederick had placed him in, yet it managed to elude him despite his best efforts.

The emperor wanted immortality, and *nothing* would stop his relentless search for it. Any day the neurotic, decrepit ruler might decide he'd had enough of his current right-hand man.

As things stood, their relationship suited Maxim. He commanded respect, or at least fear, throughout the palace, and had luxurious chambers in which to live. But things could not stay that way forever, and Maxim's schemes were going slightly awry.

For the moment, it worked well enough to help Frederick on his mad quest, until such time as Maxim had his plans in place; to keep his position and power whether the emperor was alive or not. But he was not ready for that yet, not by a long way. He saw that maybe the book was the answer to his problems, one way or another.

"You say you can divine the future?" Frederick asked. He didn't do it directly, but spoke through Maxim.

Maxim repeated the emperor's question, and the man eagerly nodded.

"Oh yes," he said. "Oh yes!"

"Very well," said Frederick to Maxim. "See what he can do."

"The emperor wishes to see an example of your skill," Maxim said.

"Very well. Of course!" the man said, looking a little nervous. He began to rummage in his bag and pulled out a tray and some cups.

"I will ask one of you," he said, speaking very quickly, 'to hide this ball beneath one of the cups and—"

"Enough," said the emperor quietly.

Maxim stepped forward.

"Stop!" he said to the man. "We have enough prestidigitators already. We are seeking genuine clairvoyant ability. You will have to do better than this. Let me show you."

Maxim called to the back of the court.

"Wolfram! Come here!"

A murmur spread through the room as the crowds

parted to let a strange-looking man walk forward to the dais where Frederick sat. He was dressed very plainly, and wore a cap with brown feathers poking out of it. He mumbled to himself as he walked. He was one of the seers of the court, whose occupation was to scry the future for Frederick. This particular seer must have been reasonably good, for he had been in court for several years. The less accurate tended to vanish, quickly.

"Sire?" he said, without emotion.

Frederick nodded at Maxim.

Maxim turned back to the applicant.

"You say you can foretell the future. So tell us. What is going to happen to you in the next five minutes?"

The man dropped his bag, and wiped his forehead.

"I . . . I don't . . . ," he began, then steadied himself. "I mean, I think I will be happy to accept your generous offer of a position in your command."

He forced a wide smile.

Maxim turned to the seer.

"Seer?" he asked.

For the first time a glimmer of emotion showed on Wolfram's face. He shut his eyes and a frown developed. He opened his eyes, now moist, but it was a flat, almost disembodied, voice that spoke to Maxim.

"He will die."

That was all. He turned and shambled back into the crowd.

"Ha!" said Frederick. "Correct! He is correct!"

The man began to protest.

"You can't do that. He can't . . . It's a set-up! You can't just kill me. . . ."

He stepped forward and pulled a knife from inside his tunic. Instantly, without fuss, two guards closed in on him and slew him where he stood.

"Silly man," said Frederick. "Oh, do take him away. Don't just stand there! He's bleeding on my carpets."

Maxim sighed. It was a scene he had seen too often to find amusing anymore.

His thoughts turned back to the strange boy in the dungeon.

10

As soon as the blind jailer left, Boy wasted no time.

He'd come back with more slop, and more oil for the lamp, having finally smelt that it had gone out.

He was in no particular hurry as he lowered the lamp on its long chain from the center of the ceiling, and poured more oil into its base.

Boy saw a scratch of sparks away in the center of the dungeon and the lamp was lit.

The jailer hoisted it back to the ceiling, brought Boy his food and once more took a second bowl somewhere else.

Now he was gone, and Boy took out his lockpick and set himself free again. He headed straight toward the dungeon's far wall, in the direction the jailer had taken.

When Boy was a little less than halfway across, having averted his eyes from the hideous machines in the center of the room, he heard singing again. It was still faint, but now with the weak light from the lamp, Boy knew he was awake, and not merely imagining it.

He passed the center of the chamber and the oil lamp, and once he had, the blackness began to grow again. He waited to see if his eyes would get used to the deepening gloom, and after a moment, went on.

The singing grew louder. It was a man's voice but it was high and wavering.

"Hello?" Boy called.

Nothing, except the singing. Now he could make out some of the words, and without consciously realizing it, they felt familiar to him.

> "Surely you won't run,
> When your boat is ready to sail.
> Surely you will stand
> And face the gentle rain?"

Then he saw something. A pinprick of light, so tiny at first he couldn't be sure it wasn't his eyes playing a trick on him. As he stepped toward it, however, the light grew in size. It was still small, but it was bright, and shone like a jewel through the deepness of the dark in the dungeon.

He moved closer and came to a row of cells that he had not seen before. They were like his own, set into the wall in a row of four or five.

Beyond them lay the light, and now Boy saw it was a window cut through the solid rock, very small, just wider than a couple of hands. It was divided in four by a sturdy iron cross, so not even Boy would have been able to get more than a few fingers through its gaps.

He went closer, and still the singing continued.

> "In the morning you should think
> You might not last unto the night,
> In the evening you should think

You might not last unto the morn.
So dance, my dears, dance,
Before you take the dark flight down."

"Hello?" Boy said. He knew this had to be where the jailer was taking the other bowl of food.

"Hello?" He tried again.

Still nothing. He had to go closer.

He realized he was breathing light and fast, taking short uneven gulps of air. To compensate, his heart began to beat faster too, trying to get enough air into his body. He was arm's length from the window now. It was slightly above his head, and as he approached, he put out a trembling hand to the grille. He stood on tiptoe to peer inside, and a warm orange light like fire spilled across his face. He had been holding his breath, but what he saw on the other side of the window took that breath clean away.

It was a room, of decent proportions, but not vast by any means. It had a low ceiling, unlike the high domed one of the dungeon, and was obviously some antechamber that had been carved from the rock. It was clearly still part of the dungeon, but there any similarity to that foul grimy place ended.

The room was beautiful. Light came from two oil lamps, one on a small table, the other hanging from the ceiling. Thick rugs lay on the floor, hiding the bare rock beneath. It was exquisitely furnished. There was a writing desk with an upholstered chair, a small but ornate bed covered in sumptuous sheets and plump pillows, red and gold. There were two wardrobes and a chest of drawers, again all of the finest quality. A small mirror with an enormously intricate gold frame hung on one wall, above a washstand with a fine porcelain bowl and a jug to match. There was even a small fireplace, with a chimney that must have been bored right through the bedrock all the way up to the palace and eventually away to the cold City air, for the room was completely free of smoke and the fire was drawing well.

Boy's eyes widened in wonder, and then he saw him.

The man who had been singing.

He was sitting in a low armchair, by the fire. Boy tried to speak again, and the words caught in his mouth.

But he had been seen.

"Don't ask me for food. I ate it all. You can't have mine."

Boy was still too stunned to speak.

The man went back to his singing. Boy struggled to think what to say, what to ask, but he was distracted by the song. He knew it. He knew it, but could not remember where from.

"Who are you?"

It was a simple question, but the man seemed confused.

He looked up at Boy, then into the fire. He did not reply.

"I'm Boy," said Boy. "My name . . . is Boy. Who are you?"

The man looked back at Boy. He was old, quite tall, and had probably even been strong once upon a time. He wore a short gray pointed beard, and his features were fine, though his eyes seemed dead.

"Me?" he asked. "Me? I . . . can't remember."

He stopped, looked around again.

Boy stuttered another question.

"Wh-What are you doing down here?"

As soon as it was uttered, he realized his question was foolish, and asked another.

"Are you in charge here? Do you look after the prisoners?"

The man started to laugh, softly at first, and then more and more loudly.

"Prisoners?" he said. "What prisoners? I am the only one down here now."

Boy shook himself. His feet were aching from standing on tiptoe at the small window. He looked around, to see if there was a door that led into the chamber, but could see nothing. He tried to pull himself up with his fingers again to make it easier.

"How long?" asked Boy. "When did they put you down here?"

The man blinked at Boy.

"I don't know what you mean."

Boy felt a shuddering fear take hold of him. The man couldn't remember his own name, and Boy couldn't understand how you could forget your name, if you were lucky enough to have one. Unless it had been a long time since anyone had used it. Boy's question about time had thrown the man too. Just how long had he been moldering in the dungeon?

But something didn't make sense. If this man was a prisoner, why was he living in luxury? Why the fine clothes and furnishings? If it was a prison, it was a strange, gilded cage.

"Why are you down here?" Boy asked.

"Too long ago," said the man, obliquely.

Now he asked Boy a question.

"What did you say your name was?"

"I'm called Boy and I've got to get out of here."

"I haven't seen anyone else here in a long time," the man said. "They don't keep prisoners anymore. They have other uses for them. . . ."

"What do you mean?" Boy asked.

"It's been a long time since they've had anyone here. They don't usually bother waiting . . . just take them straight to it. I expect they'll be taking you down soon, though."

"What do you mean? What is it?"

"You don't know?" asked the man. "You don't know?"

He stopped, and in the silence Boy could hear himself struggling to breathe.

"You don't know?" the man repeated. "Then I fear for you. But maybe it's best you don't know what's going to happen."

"What is it?" asked Boy, urgently. "Tell me!"

Boy pressed his face against the iron cross in the little window.

"Please!" he begged. "What is it? What is it? An animal?"

"No!" said the man. "Not an animal. It's a thing. A living thing, but they call it the Phantom."

And Boy now knew it was the thing from his nightmares, the thing lurking at the foot of the dark flight down. The Phantom.

"He's coming to take the bowl away," the man said casually. "He'd better not find you here!"

Confused, Boy said nothing.

"The jailer's coming. For the bowl."

He nodded at the table, where the empty bowl lay.

"Get away from the window!" he whispered.

As he did so, Boy saw a door on the far wall of the chamber open; the only way into this room was from the corridor outside.

He ducked down, out of sight, and realized that if the jailer had come for the man's empty bowl he would be coming for Boy's next.

He crouched low and sprinted as quietly as he could back to his own cell, determined to visit the man again as soon as he could.

Boy was alone again. Thoughts whirled through his mind. Thoughts of the days he'd spent with Valerian, dark days before the end, of the trip to the Trumpet, where a man had been slain, and of Willow finding Korp's body in the secret room in the theater. A victim of the Phantom.

The Phantom, which had been terrorizing the City for years.

The Phantom, in whose domain Boy now found himself trapped.

11

Far up above the dark catacomb in which Boy lay, the snow still fell on the City, a flake here and there sparkling in the flickering torchlight that spilled over the palace walls.

Down in the dungeons, Boy waited, and as soon as the jailer had gone, he stole across toward the shining window.

The man had not moved, but remained in his armchair, staring into the fire.

Boy felt awkward, as if he was spying, but he had already been noticed.

"You again? You're still here? I thought he might have taken you away."

Boy tried to ignore the implication of his words.

"What you said about the Phantom," he said, "how do you know about it? How do you know it's the same thing that's been killing in the City?"

The man looked up.

"I've been thinking," he said. "I've been thinking and I've remembered something."

"What?" Boy asked, patiently.

"I've remembered my name."

"That's good," said Boy. "What is it?"

"Bedrich," the man said. "At least, I think so."

Boy sighed.

"Well," he said, "perhaps I can call you that anyway."

The man thought about this for a while.

"Yes," he agreed. "Yes, that's a good idea. Or was it Gustav . . . ?"

"Bedrich sounds fine to me," said Boy quickly, then smiled. "I'll call you that."

Bedrich nodded, nearly smiling.

"So tell me. Tell me about the Phantom."

The half smile disappeared from Bedrich's face immediately.

"Why do you want to know?" he asked.

"I don't know . . . ," Boy said.

This was true, he realized. He hadn't actually stopped to think about it.

"But it killed someone I knew. Someone I worked for, in a way. The director of the theater where I worked with . . ."

He stopped again. There was no point telling this poor old man all his stories.

"So how do you know about it?"

"I look after it," Bedrich said simply.

Boy was too shocked to speak.

"I am the doctor. I am the palace doctor, you see."

"That can't be," said Boy. "I mean . . ."

"No," said Bedrich, holding up one hand. He rose from his chair and came over to the window. He inspected Boy's face closely, as if that would tell him something.

"I am the doctor, Frederick's doctor. Or rather, I was once. Now I only have one patient. The Phantom. They keep me down here for that alone. I sedate it. I try to stop it from the worst of its excesses. It's been getting harder and harder recently. I try my best, but I am not always successful.

"When I am not successful, then it needs blood. And that is why I fear for you. Though why you are not dead already, I do not know."

"But what is it?" Boy asked.

Bedrich stepped back from the window. He looked around furtively, melodramatically, though there was no one to hear him other than Boy in this subterranean prison.

"I cannot tell you."

"You mean you can't, or you won't?" Boy pressed, but Bedrich would say no more.

He turned and went back to his chair by the fire.

"Please," said Boy. "Please tell me some more."

"I'm tired," Bedrich said. "Leave me alone."

The old man snuffled quietly to himself for some time, and then fell asleep.

Boy had no choice but to return to his cell, where he curled into a ball on the hard floor and closed his eyes.

But sleep would not come. In a way he was glad, for he sensed it would bring no relief from the nightmare he was living.

12

Next time a meal was brought, the rumble in his belly told Boy it had to be another whole day. Something else came with the food.

"You've got company," said the jailer as he rattled a key in the cell next to Boy.

Boy was amazed to see Bedrich being led into the cell. The door was shut behind him.

"No point me walking over to two sides of the place to feed you, is there?" said the jailer.

Boy looked at Bedrich. He was grateful for the company, but there was something not quite right with the jailer's explanation of why they had been put together.

For some reason, the jailer stood waiting while they both ate, and when they had finished, he took their bowls from them.

"By the way, you're to go free," he said, in an offhand manner.

Boy leapt to his feet.

"When?" he cried. "Please, when?"

The jailer tilted his head to one side.

"Not you," he said. "Him."

Boy put his hands up and lightly touched the bars of his cell. He turned to Bedrich, forcing a smile.

"Did you hear? That's good."

Bedrich had heard.

A smile washed across his face, but it was quickly followed by a frown.

He looked hard at the jailer, but it was impossible to read that blind expression.

"You mean it?" he croaked. "This isn't a trick or—"

"Do you want to argue about it?" the jailer said. "I'm sure we can change their minds if you'd rather stay."

"No!" cried Bedrich. "No! Only I just . . ."

He stopped.

Boy looked at the jailer.

"Why? Why are they letting him go? Will you ask about me? Please will you ask when I'm going to be let out?"

"No," said the jailer bluntly. "Not my business. Yours. As for him, I don't know. Maybe he's been pardoned for his crimes. Going now."

With that he went.

Bedrich called after him.

"When? When?"

There was no answer, but it seemed enough for now to know.

"Boy!" he cried. "Did you hear that, Boy? They're going to let me out!"

Boy watched Bedrich, thinking, waiting, judging. The last time they had spoken Bedrich had been surly. Boy needed Bedrich now. He needed him to speak; he needed his help.

Watching Bedrich, Boy finally remembered the song

Bedrich had been singing. It was the "Linden Song," which he and Willow and Valerian had heard the miserable cart driver sing as they hunted for the book in that desolate village in the snow-laden countryside.

Like falling snow, its words floated freely through his head now as he relived the horror of that frozen churchyard, and inside the church itself, the discovery of Gad Beebe's grave, where they had believed the book lay. And so it had, once. But someone had beaten them to it. Kepler.

It was no surprise that Boy's thoughts had drifted to the book, no surprise at all. He was sure that his destiny lay entwined with it. He knew it would hold an answer for him. If only he could get to it, there was still a chance for him.

It was no use, this nameless life. He had spent enough time as a rootless being, without home, or heritage. He had come to accept Valerian's abuse of him as normal, but Willow had shown him enough love to make him see that it was not. He had to find answers now. He needed to know who his parents were. Maybe he would never know who his mother was, but one look in the book would at least tell him the truth about Valerian.

Boy watched as all sorts of feelings passed through Bedrich's mind, as he contemplated what it would be like to be free after untold years.

"I need your help," Boy said, trying to judge Bedrich's mood. Boy was pleased to see he seemed calm.

Bedrich nodded.

"When you get out. Will you do something for me?"

Bedrich nodded again.

"Yes," he said, gently. "Of course. I'll try."

"Thank you," said Boy. "Thank you. I need you to find someone for me. And take her a message. Can you do that?"

"Oh yes," said Bedrich. "Whatever you say!"

Encouraged, Boy went on.

"I need you to find a girl, a girl called Willow. She works at an orphanage called St. Stephen's, it's run by a woman called Martha."

"Martha, Martha. Yes," said Bedrich.

"When you find Willow, tell her where I am. Tell her to steal the book and bring it here."

Bedrich looked at Boy, staring him straight in the eyes for almost the first time since they had met.

"What did you say?" he asked.

Something in his manner put Boy on his guard, instantly. He thought about what he had said.

"I said . . . tell Willow to—"

"Not that," said Bedrich. "What you said after that."

"There's . . . a book," Boy said, slowly. He had only dared talk of it to Bedrich because he believed it could mean nothing to him. "It's very powerful and—"

"And it's dangerous," said Bedrich. He held up his hand, to stop Boy from speaking. "Oh yes, I know about the book. Only I thought it had been dealt with. Long, long ago."

13

"Maxim!" yelled Frederick. "Dammit, Maxim! Where are you?"

"Coming, sire, coming!"

Frederick sat up in bed, propped on dozens of small velvet cushions. His bed was a vast thing, far too big for such a little man. In his white nightgown and nightcap he looked like a sailor marooned in a sea of silken sheets.

"Blast this bed!" he cursed. "Why can't I have something more comfortable?"

Maxim hurried from his own impressive rooms a little way down the corridor to Frederick's chambers, the most sumptuous part of the palace.

He strode down the corridor oblivious to the spectacular views across the rest of the palace, and then down over the City.

"Max-im!" screeched the emperor from his bedchamber.

Maxim rushed through the doorway and almost slipped on the ridiculously polished floor.

"Sire?" he said.

"Maxim. Why are you always so slow? Anyone would think you are trying to kill me. Don't you understand I have needs?"

"My apologies, sire," Maxim said, trying to keep any note of irritation from his voice. "I was attending to some other matters."

"Well, don't," Frederick snapped. "You attend to me and me alone."

"Indeed, sire. The matters I speak of were concerned with—"

"I'm not interested, Maxim. Understand me! Now listen. I want to see some progress. You're dragging your heels."

"Sire?" Maxim said, with too much of a question in his voice.

"Don't question me! I want to see some results! Bring the court seers to me. I want to see what they think about what you're doing. Or what you're not doing . . ."

Frederick stared straight at Maxim. The tall man looked at the floor, his eyes burning. He thought about the useless wretches Frederick insisted on maintaining at court and fumed, but he said nothing.

"You've been dragging your heels and I want results. And soon. I'm getting older by the day and I don't feel at all well. This bed hurts me, for a start. You've no conception of it. None at all."

"I will have it—"

"Just listen to me. You know what I asked you to do, so do it. If not, I'll find someone else who can. In the meantime, bring the seers to me. Let's see what they have to say. If you had only kept that boy perhaps you might have got somewhere by now."

"The . . . boy, sire? The boy from the magician's house?"

"Yes, yes, of course the boy from the magician's house.

116

Who else do you think I mean? If you hadn't had him killed . . ."

Maxim cursed the whims of the emperor, but restrained himself from saying what he really thought. He wasn't going to let this chance go by, however.

"Ah . . . but Your Highness is absolutely right. Fortunately, it was . . . not possible to dispatch the boy as *you* wished. He is still in our dungeons. . . ."

Frederick looked up at him sharply.

"As *I* wished, Maxim? As *I* wished? I made no such decision. I told you to lock him up until we were ready to see him, and you know I never change my mind! You know that to disobey me would mean your death, do you not? Is that not right?"

"No! No, sire," said Maxim, hurriedly. How was he supposed to win with this cantankerous old swine? "Of course I do everything you require of me, yet maybe I am . . . misremembering your instructions. Fortunately everything is as you wish. He is indeed incarcerated in our dungeons. If you wish to see the boy . . . ?"

"No, I do not," Frederick said. "Well, not yet. Have him cleaned and then bring him to court. Let us see what he knows. And then, if he still proves useless, you can drown him."

Maxim swore silently at the floor as he averted his face from Frederick's view once more.

"Very good, sire," he said. "At once."

He left, shutting the door behind him, just a little too hard.

14

Willow hurried through the darkening City streets yet again, headed south, over the river, her companion at her side.

Kepler.

As they crossed the wide street known as the Parade, Willow pulled her shawl about her more closely as she was struck by a sharp cold wind that sent the snowflakes into flurries.

An hour or so later they turned into a rancid little alley called the Bucket, named after a low-life drinking den halfway along it. At the far end the river lay before them.

They crossed at St. Olaf's Bridge, a fantastic span of three powerful arches, wide and noble in its construction. At each of the two piers where stone thrust its way into the riverbed, the thoroughfare widened into a bay, where the ponderous or weary might consider the flow of water and time passing below them. On each pier was a small cage, just big enough to permit a man's body to be forced inside. Willow shuddered as she passed them, but fortunately, it had been many years since they had been used.

At the far bank, the street plummeted rapidly back into

the chaos of the City's maze, and any sense of architectural order given by the bridge vanished.

But after a turn or two, there was the palace mound ahead of them, pressed against a bend in the river.

After she had bumped into Kepler by the North Gate the day before, they had returned to his house, arguing all the way. Yet each knew they needed the other.

They had made their way back across the City as fast as they could, for the night and the snow were deepening. Even without Kepler's company Willow would have known her way unerringly.

On reaching the house, Kepler had provided some bread and cheese, for which Willow was truly grateful. Kepler was an intelligent man, a great intellect, but he had seemed clumsy and slow as he prepared the food for Willow, as if it was something he never did. It was no feast, but had been enough to sustain her.

As soon as dawn had come, Kepler had collected things in a large shoulder bag, and they had set out once more for the palace.

This morning the arguments had stopped; they had barely spoken.

"We must hurry," Kepler said, as he got things together. "He's in danger there."

"I know," Willow replied.

"Do you? You don't know anything of the palace! The people inside. And there's one to be most feared."

"Who?"

"A man called Maxim. He's the emperor's right hand. He has a reputation."

"What?" asked Willow.

"It would frighten you to know, child," Kepler said.

Willow stopped and waited for Kepler to notice that she had. After a few paces he saw that she was no longer with him and turned.

"You think it will scare me?" Willow shouted. "After all I've been through?"

Kepler shook his head.

"Maybe not," he said. "But there is little to tell. Maxim is a dangerous man, with great influence over the emperor and life in court. We must be most careful of him."

"Why?" asked Willow.

"Listen, girl," Kepler snapped. "You ask too many questions. I've agreed you may be able to help me find Boy, and that's enough for now. So be silent!"

Kepler would say no more. He turned and walked on, and Willow had no choice but to follow.

Now they were deep in their own thoughts, which were more similar than they might have known. Both were thinking about Boy, though as they walked Willow glanced from time to time at Kepler's sack. They had agreed on their plan the night before, but Willow couldn't help wondering what, exactly what, it was that Kepler had brought with him.

15

Boy struggled to believe what Bedrich was saying.

"Yes, I know about the book. I thought it had been dealt with, long ago."

"How?" cried Boy. "How can you know about it?"

"I know it!" Bedrich said, firmly. "I know the book. I once looked into it myself. . . ."

He stopped, took a deep breath.

"It did me no good. It has done others much worse."

That was true. Boy thought of Valerian. The book hadn't saved him after all, though it might have done at the cost of Boy's life.

"But how?" asked Boy. "When?"

Bedrich looked at Boy, held his eyes for a long time.

"What does a poor wretch like you know about it?" he asked. "A street child like you."

Boy shook his head.

"I don't live on the streets, not anymore. I live with . . . lived with a man. A great man, called Valerian."

"The magician?" asked Bedrich, raising an eyebrow.

"You knew him?" Boy asked.

"No. Only by reputation. Fifteen, maybe twenty years ago. He was a scholar at the Academy, but was disgraced."

Boy ignored this.

"Valerian wanted the book," he said. "We searched for it. In nasty places."

"The book is power. That much I know. But why exactly did he want it?"

"He was in trouble. He . . ."

Boy stopped. It seemed impossible to explain everything that had happened in the last few weeks.

"You speak of him as if he has gone," Bedrich said. "He is dead?"

Boy nodded.

"So he didn't get the book, to save him from this trouble?"

Boy shook his head.

"No, he did get it. He did, but . . ."

"But? What happened?"

"To save himself . . . to save himself would have meant killing me. . . ."

"And he refused? What a noble gesture!"

Boy shrugged. It wasn't quite like that, but in the end Valerian *had* died instead of him. Bedrich sensed Boy's hesitation.

"But he must have been a great man, to die instead of you. Why else would he have done it?"

"He was my father," Boy said.

The words sounded strange on his lips. He knew he might be lying, that he didn't really know the truth. But it was easier to tell Bedrich that, than to have to explain it all to him.

"What a strange boy you are!" Bedrich declared.

Boy said nothing.

"So you know about the book, about its power. And its danger."

"Willow always said it was dangerous, right from the start, but I don't see why. It's full of knowledge, and knowledge is good. Valerian always said so, and he was never wrong."

"But the book is different. Maybe if it revealed the whole truth of a matter, it would be a good thing. But it does not. It is treacherous, and malevolent. It reveals only some of the truth. It shows something different to each person. Sometimes it shows nothing at all, but when it does reveal something, you have to be very careful to understand that what it is telling you is only part of the picture."

"But Willow looked into it. She looked over Valerian's shoulder, and saw he was about to try to . . ."

He stopped. He didn't want to tell Bedrich that Valerian had tried to kill him.

"What?" asked Bedrich. "What is it? Are you beginning to understand? The doubtful nature of what the book reveals, the dangers?"

Boy nodded. He was happy to change the subject. "That song you were singing. How do you know it? And how do you know about the book? I thought it was a secret."

"It was. It should have been," said Bedrich. "But things change, obviously. I know about the book, for it was once here. In the palace."

"Here?" Boy cried.

"Shhh!" Bedrich hushed him. "Not so loud. Yes, the book was here. It's all so long ago now, such a long time. It's hard to remember it all."

"Try," Boy urged. "Please, try."

Bedrich put his head in his hands briefly, then looked up at Boy, blinking.

"The book. It came here. It was brought here, to please the emperor. You won't have seen the emperor. . . ."

Boy shook his head. "No. I have. Briefly," he said. "I was amazed. I thought Maxim had to be the one in charge. Frederick doesn't look like he could be in charge of anything."

Bedrich shook his head.

"That's what you think? Then you are mistaken. He's a hard and powerful man, despite his age, despite his weaknesses."

"Some people don't even believe he's still alive. No one's seen him in years, in the City."

"They wouldn't have, he never goes outside the palace. I used to tell him he should go out. Take the air, exercise. It might have stopped him brooding over his health all the time. He was obsessed by his health. His heart, his nerves, his stomach. It was hard being his doctor, especially when he set so much store in those alchemists and necromancers of his. . . ."

Boy felt Bedrich was drifting away again.

"The book," he said. "What about the book?"

"Yes. The book. Well, in a way it's all part of the same thing. Frederick was old even then. He must be ancient by now. Even in those days he was possessed by one concern: the imperial line."

"What?" asked Boy.

"The line. He is the last of the imperial line. There is no one to succeed him when he dies. Desperate for children, but with no heir to the throne, he began to worry that he would die and leave the empire without an emperor. Empire! What nonsense! This pox-ridden city is all that's left of it. But nonetheless, all those dukes and lords were upstairs waiting to fight it out when he goes! You see?"

"Yes"—Boy nodded—"yes, but what about the book?"

"I'm getting to it," said Bedrich. "It's all part of the same thing. He was obsessed about having an heir. And everyone in court was trying to placate him, and please him, all the while hoping for favors in return, money, a title, things like that. One day, a musician arrived in court, from the countryside. A handsome man, and of reasonable breeding. He came with a song, and a present. First he sang the song, and the emperor was even gracious enough to seem to enjoy it. He must have been in a rare good mood that day."

Bedrich had closed his eyes, as if seeing the events all over again.

"And the song was a beautiful song. Beautiful but sad. He came from a musical family. Many members of his family were gifted musically, but although they were noble, they were not wealthy. But there was something else. The present. I do not know where he came upon it, but the musician had brought with him a terrible thing, though at the time it was held to be marvelous and wonderful. The book.

"And this was his present to the emperor. He was rewarded immediately with his weight in gold. And there was more to follow. As the book foretold things and they came to pass, the man and his family were rewarded with land, titles, money and more.

125

"And more than this, the emperor even took a daughter of the family as his mistress. Sophia. This was deemed a great honor to the family. She was so beautiful, and clever, too. It was she who wrote that sad song.

"And on the day . . . the day when . . ."

Bedrich stopped. He seemed to have lost his way in the story.

"Go on," Boy said, gently.

"It's so long ago," said Bedrich, but Boy could tell that this was not the reason he had stopped. "On that day. The book foretold that the emperor was indeed to father children! On that day, the man and his family were showered beyond all measure with things rich and golden. They were granted permission to build a church in their village, and the members of the family moved within court as if they were themselves royalty."

With a shock Boy realized that he was listening to something of which he knew a part.

"Tell me," he said, "what was the name of this family?"

When Bedrich opened his mouth to answer, Boy already had the same word on his lips.

"Beebe."

Boy felt his heart begin to race light and fast in his chest. He felt sick.

"Beebe," said Bedrich again. "For a while, what a great and beautiful family they were. So beautiful."

Suddenly footsteps sounded along the corridor outside the dungeon.

"They're coming to take you!" Boy whispered. "To let you out! You won't forget about Willow, will you? And the book?"

"I will have nothing to do with that book. I refuse."

"But it is my only chance. . . ."

"If that is your only chance, you have no chance," Bedrich said. "But I will find the girl. Willow."

The door began to rattle and creak open.

"All right," said Boy, "all right. But quick! Tell me what happened to the Beebes. What happened to the book's prediction?"

The jailer approached. This time two flunkeys accompanied him.

"Tell me," whispered Boy. "What happened?"

Bedrich shook his head.

"It was not to be," he said. "The prediction was . . . awry. The Beebes were disgraced. The emperor blamed them for what had happened. Stripped them of almost everything. The book ruined them. It will ruin you too, if you let it."

The jailer was at the cells.

"Getting friendly, are we?" he said, blankly. "That's a shame. Time for you to go."

Bedrich stood up. Boy could feel the tension, the anxiety in him. After so long, to be nearly free was almost too much.

But the jailer walked to Boy's cell and stuck his key in that lock instead.

"You," he said. "You're to go with these men. Any trouble and you'll be back down here before you can breathe."

Boy didn't move.

"But what about me?" Bedrich said.

The two men moved into Boy's cell and started to walk him out of the dungeon.

"Maxim's coming to see to you," the jailer said to Bedrich.

"To set me free?" Bedrich cried, desperately. "He's coming to set me free?"

As he was taken away, Boy looked back at Bedrich.

"Bedrich . . . ," he began, but there was nothing to say, and he was roughly dragged forward.

The door swung shut behind him, and he heard Bedrich call out to the jailer.

"He's going to let me out—isn't he?"

The echoes of his voice were cut short by the door clanging back into its iron frame.

"Right," said one of the men to Boy. "Upstairs with you. One stupid move and I'll break your neck."

Bedrich sat down on the cold stone floor of the cell. His gilded cage had been taken from him, and the promise of release too. His head was so full of this misery that he didn't even notice a small spyhole swinging shut in the ceiling just above his head.

The Place of Treacherous Artifice

❧

1

Boy was hurried through the dark and twisting corridors of the dungeons once more, so cramped in places that even he, with his skinny frame, was forced to hunch up. One of the men walked in front, the other behind, prodding him in the back if he showed any signs of dawdling.

But Boy had no wish to dawdle. After one twist they came to a section of passage that Boy realized he knew. Just as in his dream, he was walking down the passage that went past the top of the steep and foul stairway down to nothingness. The smell rushed toward him, like a beast itself, assaulting his senses. He hesitated, and felt another shove in his back. Boy forced one foot after the other, and the opening to the passageway drew closer, until, holding his hand to his mouth and nose, he saw with relief that unlike in his dream, the iron gate across the opening was shut.

His captors seemed to be hurrying too.

"Is that—" he began, but was shoved again.

He stood his ground, and turned to face the man behind him.

"Is that where it lives?"

The man seemed taken aback.

"Is that where it lives?" Boy asked again.

"You shouldn't know anything about that," the guard said. Boy failed to read the meaning in his voice. Was it fear? Or surprise? It certainly wasn't anger. Boy had expected to be hit for his question, but no blow came.

The other guard had now noticed that Boy had stopped and rushed back to see what was going on.

He grabbed Boy by the neck and dragged him into walking again. He turned to his friend.

"Of all places, you want to stop here?" he said.

As they moved out of the rough-hewn, damp stone underbelly of the palace and into the royal world proper, Boy was shocked to find that it was nighttime. Having been confined for days in darkness, longing for daylight, he had assumed that when he was freed from the twilight world, the sun would be shining.

The palace seemed to be asleep; there was very little noise from anywhere, and they saw no one as they moved through lavish paneled corridors into ever more marvelous chambers.

Boy stared about him.

Never in his life had he seen such wealth, such casual displays of incredible finery at every turn. Portraits in oil hung in gilded frames. Faces peered back from the paintings, haughty figures swathed in fur robes and dripping with jewels. The floor Boy was walking on was marble; marble pillars struck from floor to the high vaulted ceiling. The walls between were paneled wood painted a pale, pale green, the details picked out with gold. Boy stared open-mouthed at the carved wooden frieze above this paneling that ran the length of the room. Whole forests were depicted in high relief, trees and bushes, with animals peeping from behind, a bird pecking at a bunch of grapes, a swan gliding on a lake.

And this was just one of the galleries down which they had passed.

Boy faltered, unable to take in what he was seeing, but he was quickly moved on by yet another poke in his back.

"Come on, boy. I want to get to bed."

"Where are we going?" asked Boy.

"Up here," one of them said, as they turned toward a massive stone staircase that swept up and around out of sight above their heads.

Boy began to walk forward, but was stopped.

"Not there!" the guard snapped. "Here."

He pulled a section of the paneling away to expose a hidden staircase, tiny and twisting, that led up out of the hall.

"Move!

Boy rushed into the tight stairwell before they could hit him again. A hand pushed him as the guards hurried up behind him. He sped up, growing dizzy as the spiral staircase twisted up and up into the palace. It was getting darker with each turn, and Boy was guessing where his next footfall would be, when he stumbled out into a dazzlingly bright room.

He blinked, heard the door click shut behind him and a key turn in a lock. When he looked around, there was no sign of the stairway from which he had emerged, nor, for that matter, was there any sign of the guards.

He was alone.

2

The room was small, though still every bit as opulent as the rest of the palace. Boy could see closed doors leading off at every side, but on one wall a set of double doors lay tantalizingly open.

Boy moved into the room beyond. In it he found a huge four-poster bed, with mattresses so deep their top was chest height from the floor. Swags of midnight blue and yellow velvet hung from the bed's canopy. It looked incredibly inviting. Who was lucky enough to sleep in such a wonderful thing?

He stepped toward it. Then he heard water splashing. Turning, he saw a small door leading out of the bedroom. Cautiously he pushed it open with his fingertips.

The door swung lightly away from him.

"Hello?" he ventured quietly.

He took a step inside.

A woman turned to face him.

Boy was shocked to see she was blind, like his jailer. She was an old woman, and yet Boy could see that her blindness was from some awful accident, not due to her age. With disgust he wondered if many servants close to Frederick's secrets were made blind.

"Oh!" she said. "You're here sooner than they told me. Your bath isn't quite ready yet."

She carried on with her work. Boy took a step farther into the room. It was every bit as large as the bedroom, but in the center of it stood not a bed, but a large marble bath, carved to look like a porpoise breaking the surface of the sea. The bath itself was hollowed into its back.

The woman was busy pouring buckets of water into the tub. She had two, one with cold and one with steaming hot water. When they were empty she took them to the side of the room, lifted a hatch and placed them on a shelf inside. She pulled a bell-rope beside the hatch, and immediately the shelf dropped from view. A minute or so later, the shelf rose back into view, jerking slowly to its former position. She hoisted the buckets off deftly, and Boy saw that once again they were full of water, one hot, one cold.

He had never seen such sophistication. Bathing was something he did only very rarely. When he had lived on the streets he had only washed in summer, just to cool down, by running through one of the City's cleaner fountains. At the Yellow House, Valerian had made him wash once a week, "whether you need to or not." But this had meant a cold slosh of water in a basin, a thing as far removed from the elaborate display before him as was possible.

"You—you must have the wrong idea . . . ," Boy stammered. "You can't mean me."

"This is your bath, these are your rooms," said the woman. "Couple more buckets should do you."

"I don't understand," Boy said. "I've been in the dungeon.

They had me locked up in the dungeon. This can't be for me."

"The emperor wants to see you. You can't appear before an emperor smelling like that."

She didn't smile, or indeed betray any emotion, merely poured the last of her buckets into the vast bathtub.

"The emperor?" asked Boy. "What does he want to see me for?"

The woman didn't answer.

"Well, anyway, I don't want to see him. If you'll excuse me. I don't mean to be rude . . ."

Boy turned to leave. The woman made no effort to stop him, but he ran from the bathroom back through the bedroom. Choosing a door at random, he burst from the room, and ran straight into a guard who was almost larger than the doorway. Boy bounced off, and landed on his backside.

The guard, who barely seemed to have noticed, turned and looked down at Boy menacingly.

"Sorry," said Boy, "wrong door."

He got up, and shut himself back into his magnificent prison.

The old servant was waiting for him.

"The other doors are exactly the same," she said. "Have a bath. Go to bed. In the morning you're to go before the emperor."

"And food?" asked Boy. "Can I have something to eat? I've only had—"

"It's on its way. But bath first. You could smell better, that's for sure. Take your clothes off."

Boy gave up. He started to pull his shirt off, and the

woman left the room. He shook his head. She was kinder than the old blind man but nonetheless she was just as much his jailer.

As soon as Boy was naked he stepped into the water. It was very hot, and he had to lower himself slowly into the tub, bit by bit. He thought he had never felt water so hot. He got as far as putting his legs in, and noticed they were turning pink from the heat. Eventually he got all of himself into the bath, and lay back. He watched the steam rising all around him, and felt his eyelids begin to droop.

In another few seconds, he was asleep.

When he woke, he felt terrible. He had no idea how long he had been asleep, but the water was still warm, so it couldn't have been too long.

"Your food's here," said a voice.

He jerked upright to see the old serving woman sitting on a chair at the far side of the room.

"You better eat it and get to bed," she said. "What's this, by the way?"

Boy saw what she was holding in her hands; his lock-pick, the old metal tendon.

"I found it in your clothes," she said, needlessly. "I was going to throw it away, but then I thought maybe it's something valuable, or important. Is it important?"

Boy struggled for an answer.

"Yes," he said. "Well, no. It's only important to me. It's . . . a lucky charm. Had it for years."

The woman considered this. A frown crossed her face.

"I'm not supposed to . . . ," she began. "But I don't see it can do any harm. You can keep it."

And with that she left the room. A moment later she came back carrying a large towel and a nightshirt.

Boy grabbed the towel and pulled it around him.

They moved into the bedroom, where a table had been laid so that it was overflowing with delightful, delicate things to eat. Once again Boy was amazed, having never seen such things in all his life.

"Don't eat too quickly," the woman said, but Boy ignored her. He sat down and began to devour everything he could, not even stopping to ask what some of it was.

The serving woman sat quietly on a chair, half a smile flickering across her face all the time, listening to Boy eat.

"My!" she said, when he began to slow down. "You were hungry, weren't you."

For a moment, Boy felt like shouting at her. How stupid was she not to know the kind of slop he'd been given to eat for days? Of course he was hungry.

"Are you going to hang around while I do everything?" he asked, instead.

"Sorry," she said. "Only it's been a while since we've had anyone up here in the Winter Rooms."

Boy wondered who "we" was.

"And your guests?" Boy asked. "Are they always prisoners? Like me?"

"Don't say that. We try to make things as good as we can for our guests while they're here. . . ."

She trailed off, then stood to go.

"Eat up and go to sleep," she said.

Boy looked at the bed. It was so tall there was a little ladder to take him up onto it.

He slipped under the sheets, but something was not

right. As he had had trouble adjusting to the comfortable yet small bed in Kepler's house after the rotten cot he'd had at Valerian's, he could not feel comfortable in this enormous bed.

He got up, and standing on the bed, pulled at the swags of velvet and drew them together like curtains, so that he was enclosed on all sides. It was immediately a dark and much smaller space, and feeling more at home, Boy shut his eyes, thoughts of Valerian drifting through his mind as he made his way down to sleep.

Despite the late, late hour, not everyone in the palace was asleep. The old serving woman made her way wearily to her own modest room on the floor above the one where Boy was dozing. In the kitchens in the North Wing, servants were still scrubbing and scraping at pots, and farther down into the palace's guts, a tall figure robed in red made his way back from the dungeons. Once again there had been difficult work to be done down there, and there was more ahead.

3

Boy was pulled from his bed by a hand at his throat before he was even awake. He fell to the ground and lay spluttering on the thick, soft carpet that surrounded the massive four-poster.

"No more lying!" Maxim shouted down at him.

Boy didn't even have time to think, let alone answer, before Maxim snatched him up from the floor and flung him across the room. Fortunately almost all of the bedroom floor was covered by one plush rug or another, and he was not hurt.

Now at some distance from Maxim, he had time to think before another blow came.

"Wait!" Boy cried. "What are you talking about? I don't even know what you're talking about!"

Maxim stopped halfway across the room.

"Then let me remind you," he said. He ran one hand over the top of his smooth head. "You recall our last conversation?"

Boy frowned.

"You were asking me—"

"About a book," Maxim spat. "About *the* book. Yes?"

Now Boy panicked. He couldn't remember exactly what he'd said. He needed to lie consistently if he was going to bluff his way out of this.

"Oh. Yes," said Boy. "Yes, you were asking about Valerian's books. Have you found what you needed?"

Boy realized as soon as he said it that it was a mistake. Maxim closed the distance between them, and though Boy flinched, he still took most of a blow to the side of his head.

He fell to the ground, holding his head, feeling for blood, though there was none. Maxim yanked Boy to his feet and pushed his face close.

"Listen, Boy. Listen!" he snarled. "I know you are lying. I know you have the book somewhere. So make an end to your foolishness."

"N-No . . . ," stuttered Boy. "No, I don't. . . ."

"Yes, you do. You have the book. Or maybe it is your friend Willow who has it now?"

Boy's face betrayed him immediately.

"Willow!" he cried, and then knew that Maxim somehow knew the truth.

"Yes, your friend Willow," said Maxim, smoothly. He dropped Boy back to the floor, went to fetch a chair and brought it back to sit on. "Let's have a little talk, shall we? Now that we understand each other. And now that you see it is pointless to lie anymore."

"Willow's got nothing to do with all this. You don't—"

"I decide what is important here. Understand me! Your conversations with your friend Bedrich were very helpful.

You were much more forthcoming with him than you have been with me so far."

Boy's thoughts whirled as he struggled to understand, but it was obvious that Maxim had somehow been listening to them. He tried to remember what he and Bedrich had talked about, but he knew it was not good.

Everything. They had talked about everything.

"Yes, it was good of you two to become such friends after I had you put next to each other. And when you saw the chance to get a message out, you kindly took it. . . ."

Maxim laughed, and Boy saw that the whole of his imprisonment had been a trick to get him to talk to Bedrich. It had seemed strange that the old doctor had been moved in next to him.

Sickeningly Boy realized that in talking to Bedrich he had exposed Willow to danger too. He cursed himself.

"What have you done to Bedrich?" Boy asked.

"He is well enough, for the time being."

They needed him alive, Boy realized, to look after the Phantom. That was something else about Bedrich's release that hadn't made sense, but the prisoners had been too preoccupied with their own thoughts to see it at the time.

"What's going to happen to me?" Boy asked, miserably.

"Silence!" Maxim shouted. "Just tell me this: Where is the book? Does your friend Willow have it?"

"No!" cried Boy.

"You're lying again! You will die if you persist. Are you that stupid? The girl has the book! Where is she?"

"No, no, she doesn't!" cried Boy. "Really. Please believe me."

Maxim said nothing, obviously trying to weigh up the truth or otherwise of Boy's words.

"Why should I believe you?"

"It's the truth, I swear it's the truth," Boy said, hurriedly. "I don't know where the book is. I don't know where Willow is. . . ."

"Come now," said Maxim. "You know your friend Willow is at the orphanage."

Boy felt sick again.

"Yes," said Maxim. "You are right. I do have my men going there right now. So maybe we'll find the book sooner than I had hoped."

"No!" cried Boy. "She doesn't have the book!"

"Then who does? If your girl doesn't have it then who does? Tell me that!"

"I don't know," said Boy. He dared not mention Kepler.

"Then maybe Willow will be more helpful than you have been," Maxim said. "And believe me, I am in no mood to reward unhelpful people, so think carefully about what you choose to say from now on. In ten minutes we are due in court, where you will confirm everything I say to the emperor. About the book, about the magician, about your friend. If you make the slightest mistake, I will have you back in the dungeon, but not for long. Perhaps you have seen a certain dark stairway, a flight down to the very depths of Hell? That is where you will be headed, my lying little Boy, if you make one more mistake. And your stay there will be a short one, believe me. Believe me."

He pointed at another chair, on which some new clothes lay.

"Get dressed," he said. "I will come back for you in ten minutes. And remember, your first mistake in court will be your last."

4

Once more Boy was simply awestruck by what he saw around him.

He had never seen anything like the court before, never even imagined that anything so beautiful, so majestic, so elaborate could exist. How could he? He whose life had been spent on the streets, whose only contact with wealth had been on those occasions when he relieved some care-less rich person of their purse.

It was not only the setting, but the people, dressed in magnificent clothes, with sculpted hair, or in some cases flamboyant wigs, and more jewelry than Boy had seen in his whole life.

Boy had scratched at his new clothes as Maxim had walked him down to court. They were stiff, heavy, formal clothes for a young man of the palace, and Boy did not like them, but as he stood in court for the first time he forgot all about them. His jaw dropped as he stared at everything, from the shining stone floor covered in thick rugs, to the arched ceiling far above his head, painted with heavenly scenes, rich in blue and gold. Boy was so busy staring at everything that he didn't even notice that everyone else was staring at him. Hushed conversations flurried around the room.

"Shut your mouth, Boy," Maxim whispered as Frederick arrived.

Frederick was brought into the court on a low chair carried by four men. They placed him at the foot of the dais on which his throne stood, and they and everyone else in the room bowed as the small, old, thin man climbed up into his seat of power like a toddler climbing onto his father's lap.

The proceedings began.

"Where is the boy?" Frederick drawled.

Maxim grabbed Boy by his elbow, holding it so tightly it hurt, then marched him forward. Boy felt the eyes of everyone in the room fixed on him alone as he approached the throne. Everyone except the emperor, whose face was turned to the ceiling.

"Why do we have to do everything so early?" he whined.

"Sire, it is nearly midday . . . ," Maxim said, in as gentle a tone as he could muster.

"When will you learn that this palace exists to operate around the hours I wish to keep? And not any other way?"

Boy was almost embarrassed by the old man's bickering in front of all the nobles, but the emperor was oblivious. Maxim was so used to these debates that he paid little attention, yet Boy found it utterly strange.

"This is the brat?" Frederick asked, still not actually looking at Boy.

Maxim nodded.

"Indeed, sire. He goes by a rather strange name. His name is Boy."

There was a titter around the court and Boy felt himself flush with shame, and anger too.

Finally Frederick seemed to be interested in something.

"His name is Boy? How peculiar. Did the magician not give him a proper name?"

"Apparently he did not see fit to do so," Maxim intoned slowly.

There was another giggle around the room, and Boy could stand it no more.

"That's not—" he began, but Maxim grasped his neck. The wind was plucked from his throat, and though Maxim let him go almost as fast as he had grabbed him, for a moment Boy was unable to speak.

"Very well," Frederick muttered. "It matters not. What news is there? Does he have the secret?"

"Things are proceeding very well," Maxim declared. "As Boy will testify. The book will shortly be in our possession, and when it is, we will be able to attend to your immediate situation, just as you desire."

Frederick did not seem impressed.

"Even now," Maxim went on, "my men are closing in on the book. The boy has informed me of its whereabouts. It will be here before the day is out!"

Boy wondered how Maxim dare take such a risk. Did he really believe it? Maybe he was playing for time.

Where was Willow? He hoped to God it was nowhere near the orphanage. One thing was sure, the men of the Imperial Guard would not find the book there. At least it was safe with Kepler, and it seemed Maxim knew nothing about him. If Maxim got hold of the book, not only would he wield terrible power in the palace, putting all their lives at risk, but Boy's chance of using it would be gone too.

Boy snapped out of his musings. He realized the whole court was staring at him again. He looked at Maxim, who was glaring down at him.

"Is that not so?" Maxim asked, meaningfully.

Boy understood that this was his moment, when he had to confirm everything Maxim had claimed.

"Yes," he blurted out, almost shouting. "Yes. The book. Yes."

Frederick nodded, and smiled mirthlessly.

"Very well," he said. "For both your sakes I hope you're right. Now let us get on with the day's business. . . ."

Maxim moved round to the side of the dais and motioned for Boy to follow.

There were a small commotion and a short fanfare, and then someone called out.

"Applicants for positions in the royal palace!"

Maxim hissed to Boy where he stood at his side.

"Be quiet. Watch and say nothing. You have done enough for one day."

Boy did as he was told. He had obviously slept late into the day, as Maxim had told Frederick it was midday. He had eaten far too much too quickly and his dreams had been strange affairs once more. Bits of them came back to him now as he vaguely watched what was going on in court. He had been crawling down a tunnel too low to stand upright in, and there had been something he had been trying to get to. He struggled to remember. Then it came back to him—not something, but someone. Willow. She had been at the end of the tunnel, but no matter how far he crawled, she remained as far away as ever.

In the court, a man in black stepped forward. Several other applicants had been curtly dismissed already, and Maxim was glad that the emperor was not in a murderously vindictive frame of mind on this particular day. The man in black announced, "Your Majesty, I am an alchemist."

Frederick stared at the ceiling.

"Really?" he said. "Prove it! And quickly. My legs are beginning to ache sitting here all the time. . . ."

The man bowed.

"Of course!" he said. "My things!"

He called to the back of the room, where some flunkeys had been holding his equipment. In a few minutes he had set up a burner over which sat a tripod.

He began to rummage in a bag, and pulled out a little stone crucible.

"I will now turn a small quantity of lead into gold, in this alchemical wonder, the secret system, the torment of the metals, the genesis through the twenty-seven transformations . . ."

Boy, who had become interested in the goings-on, muttered to himself.

"It's a trick."

"Be quiet," Maxim said, but Frederick leaned round in his throne.

"What did he say?"

"Nothing," Maxim replied.

"I want to hear what the boy said," Frederick said to Maxim acidly. "What did you say, Boy?"

Boy hesitated.

"What did you say? Tell me!"

"I said it's a trick."

"How do you know?" Frederick asked, carefully.

The man in black seemed to hesitate. He opened his mouth to speak, and Frederick, not even looking in his direction, held up his hand.

"One more word from you and I'll have you killed right now."

So, thought Boy, the old emperor was sharp when he wanted to be.

"Now, Boy. Tell me how you know it's a trick," Frederick said.

"It's a stage trick. The crucible has a false bottom, made of wax. When it heats up, the wax melts and there's gold underneath already."

There was a gasp around court and everyone began to speak at once.

"The brat lies!" cried the alchemist, but before he could defend himself, Maxim snatched the crucible from the man's hand. He scratched inside it rapidly with his fingernail.

He held the crucible in the air, turning it over, showing the insides first to the assembly in court, and then to Frederick. Flakes of wax fell to the floor.

From the base of the small crucible came the unmistakable glint of gold.

The room fell silent.

"Kill him," said Frederick.

"No!" cried Boy. "You can't kill him just for that, you can't!"

But no one paid Boy any attention, except Maxim, who walked over and clapped his hand across Boy's mouth.

Boy turned away as the man was led struggling from the room. He wrestled with Maxim, pulling his hand away from his mouth.

"I didn't mean for that to happen. I . . . You can't kill him."

Maxim grasped Boy again and squeezed his throat.

"One mistake, Boy. Remember, one mistake."

Boy fell silent.

The man had been an impostor, a trickster, but that was surely not reason enough to kill him? Boy had done much worse in his time. Much worse.

Frederick turned to Boy.

"Excellent Boy!" he cried. "Well done! You have proved yourself a worthy young man already! Don't you think so, Maxim? Eh, Maxim? Clever Boy. We shall have to look after him. Eh, Maxim?"

Maxim forced a smile.

"Indeed," he said.

"Worth keeping him after all, eh? You should take more notice of what I say, Maxim, then we might be closer to our goal!"

Maxim forced another thin smile, but in his eyes there was only anger, thinly veiled.

Boy said nothing, but watched the emperor grinning at him stupidly, nodding in appreciation. He felt wretched for the alchemist in black. If not for Boy, he'd be alive.

"Next!" called a footman, and the crowd parted as the last applicants of the day took the risk of applying for favors within the royal palace.

A man and a boy, both wearing hooded capes, made their way forward to the front of the court.

They removed their hoods and Boy saw that the smaller figure was not a boy but a girl. A man and a girl.

Kepler and Willow.

5

"They had better be good," Maxim muttered to Boy. "Whoever they are they had better be good. Once he's in the mood for blood . . ."

Boy looked at Willow.

Yes, she had seen him, he could tell, from the way she was looking anywhere but at him. It was the same with Kepler. Both of them were studiously avoiding eye contact with him. He understood what it meant. Say nothing, do nothing to give us away. But Boy desperately needed to warn them.

They didn't know that their lives hung by a thread, and that if they failed to impress the emperor, their end would have come.

Boy tried to catch Willow's eye, but she was having none of it. She gazed straight ahead, paying attention only to Kepler when necessary. Boy tried to twitch his head to get her attention, but Maxim saw him.

"What are you doing, idiot? Be still. They're the last for today, then you can go to your rooms until we have the book."

Boy stood still, shut his eyes and prayed.

"What do you have to show us?" Maxim asked Kepler.

Kepler stepped forward.

"I am Arbronsius!" he declared. "This is my assistant, Mina."

He indicated Willow with a flourish of his hand.

"We have come far to your great City to demonstrate our mystical powers to Your Highness."

"Get on with it, man," Frederick barked.

Wordlessly Boy urged Kepler to hurry up. The old lunatic might have them killed for taking too long.

"Indeed," Kepler said, searching in a bag at his feet. "I just need some equipment. . . ."

"Equipment? Equipment?" snapped Frederick. "You're not some confounded telescopist, are you? Can't stand those upstarts!"

"No, indeed, no," Kepler said hurriedly. "I have no truck with those modern natural philosophers, those scientists, treacherous telescopists!"

He sounded unconvincing to Boy, but then only Boy and possibly Willow knew that that was precisely what he was, a scientist, albeit one whose mind had definitely been influenced by the finding of the book. But Frederick and the rest of the court seemed to have believed him, as he bent down once more and pulled some things from his bag.

"No, sire, this is a truly magical appurtenance which I hold before you."

With a flourish worthy of Valerian, Kepler pulled a short brass cylinder from his sack. Immediately Boy recognized it as the lens from the camera obscura, upon the end of which was mounted a frosted glass tube.

"Behold," Kepler said dramatically, "the Spirit Tube."

Frederick stifled a yawn with the back of his hand.

"The Spirit Tube is a conduit through which we can see the spirit world. Sometimes we are lucky enough to capture visions of this other world inside. Allow me to attempt a summoning!"

Kepler passed the device over for Willow to hold, while he moved his hands around it. He began to mutter under his breath, not loudly enough for anyone to hear. Boy was surprised. He had never imagined that Kepler could equal Valerian's ability for performing, yet that was precisely what he was doing. Boy knew Kepler had no magical powers, was a scientist pure and simple, yet as he watched, Kepler made a very fair show of playing the magician.

For a while nothing happened; then the tube began to glow with a yellowish green light, soft and sickly. Kepler held the tube high above his head for everyone to see, and then there was a gasp as people saw a face appear through the glow inside the tube.

Now Boy knew what he was seeing—it was basically the same trick Valerian had used to summon the fairy in his hands for the first part of the Fairyland Vanishing Illusion, his most famous trick. Perhaps this was something Kepler had shown him too. A question arose in Boy's mind. Was this why Kepler had sent him to the Yellow House to fetch the lens? Had he had this in mind even then?

"The Spirit Tube!" Kepler cried, then dropped it to the floor. The light disappeared, and he bowed at Frederick, praying he had done enough.

"Sometimes," he added, rising again, "we even hear voices from the other realm!"

Boy held his breath, hardly daring to look at Frederick. Willow stood a little behind Kepler, stone still.

Frederick stood and pointed at Kepler.

"Excellent!" he declared, looking like a spoilt little boy. "Don't you think so, Maxim?"

"Very impressive," said Maxim coolly.

"Yes, very," said Frederick, turning back to Kepler. "What was your name again?"

"Arbronsius," Kepler said. "And this is Mina."

"Very good, very good. You may take rooms in the palace, and you can show us more of your learning, by and by."

"Thank you, sire," Kepler said, bowing low. As he stood up he shot a glance at Boy, who nodded, ever so slightly.

Boy looked from Kepler to Willow, and saw the faintest trace of a smile cross her lips.

6

Boy was back in his chambers in the Winter Rooms. A different servant from last time was tidying, and clearing away the meal Boy had just eaten. She was young, and Boy had been relieved to see that she at least was not blind. He stood at the window, ignoring her, trying to get some bearings of the palace, trying to work out where his room was in relation to the rest of it, but it proved difficult.

After a while, he stopped thinking about the geography of the palace, and watched the snow fall once more. His nerves were ragged, he felt edgy and scared. Seeing Willow again, here, in the heart of danger, unnerved him. He not only had to worry about getting himself out, now he had to worry about her as well. He knew she was safe from Maxim's men, but what would happen when they returned from the orphanage empty-handed?

At least the emperor liked him, but there was small consolation in that. Boy had seen how his mood might change on a whim.

Boy watched another flake of snow drift past the window, and automatically began to count, feeling a little calmer with every flake that fell.

He had no idea where Kepler and Willow were now.

They had been led away in quite a different direction from the one he had taken to the Winter Rooms.

"Where do real guests go?" he asked the girl. "Not prisoners like me."

The girl stopped her work and looked puzzled.

"If I was a proper visitor," Boy explained, "where would I stay?"

The girl thought for a moment. She showed no sign of suspicion at Boy's questions.

"It depends on who they are. Lords are put in Fountain Court, Dukes in the Western State Rooms."

"What about people like the alchemists? That kind of person."

"Oh," said the servant. "That's different. They all go to the Old South Tower."

"And where's that?"

"Long way from here," she said, turning to leave. "Across the Great Court. It's the tallest tower in the whole palace."

Boy smiled. He could do something with the information the girl had given him.

There were guards outside each of the doors, but there was the secret stairwell by which he had first arrived in his rooms. That was locked, but then the older servant had also made a mistake, by letting Boy keep his lockpick.

Boy lay on the bed, and waited for it to get dark.

7

It took Boy longer to get started than he had thought it would. Despite having first entered his chambers through the secret door, it took him half an hour of slowly search-ing the walls to find it. Even when he did he could not ac-tually be sure he had, so cleverly was it concealed.

It was not a hard lock to pick, once he managed to find the keyhole itself, which was hidden on the carved rail that ran round the room. A flick with his lockpick and the door popped open, hinged so cunningly that all the carved sections floated neatly away from their origin.

Boy made his way to his bed, and pulled some pillows to-gether, arranging them to look like a sleeping figure. He pulled the sheets over the top, and stuck the corner of his nightshirt out of one side of the bed.

It was dark outside. It was even darker in the hidden stairwell, but Boy carefully took a small oil lamp from his bedroom, and set off down the stairs. He didn't exactly have a plan. He thought it would be best to get outside, as-suming that it would be easier to find the Old South Tower from outside than to wander aimlessly through endless corridors.

At the foot of the hidden stairwell he hesitated, pressing his ear against the door, waiting to hear any kind of sound. None came, but he made himself wait for several minutes to be sure. Still nothing. He lowered the small handle and swung the door open, then, putting the lamp on the bottom step, he shut the door behind him, noting its position in the wall carefully before he did so. When the door was shut it was once again almost impossible to see.

The corridor was just as he remembered, only half lit, as most of the palace seemed to be at night. There was the grand marble staircase leading away upstairs, and, guessing that a hall of such importance had to be near an entrance to the palace, he set off for a set of doors opposite. He found himself in a slightly smaller hall beyond which he smelt the night air. There was a row of large doors right across the wall, but Boy saw a much smaller door at each end, and made for the nearer of these. He was halfway through when he saw the guard, dozing on a narrow wooden perch by the other small door. Boy hurried through and gently shut the door behind him.

He was outside. For the first time in days he breathed fresh air, and enjoyed the gentle wind that brushed his face, despite its coldness.

It was a moonless night, and Boy waited till he could see a little better before moving, but as his eyes adjusted to the dark, he saw a gray lawn in front of him.

Snow.

Snow covered everything, and was falling still. Immediately, he saw a problem: footprints. He would leave

160

footprints wherever he went, and even in the half-light he could see that the snow was untouched.

He stood on the steps of the palace for a long time, getting more agitated. He couldn't go back, and in the end decided to hope for the best. If it snowed heavily enough through the night, it might cover up any tracks he left.

Nonetheless, he kept to the sides of the buildings, it being his natural preference to cling to the shadows, and expose himself as little as possible.

He could not see the South Tower. In fact, he couldn't see anything resembling a tower at all. His view was obscured by the height of the square he was in.

Half an hour later he had worked his way past buildings great and small, along cloisters and down spiral stone staircases, over low walls and some high ones, all the while cursing the snow he had grown to love. His hands and feet were numb, and whenever he looked behind him he saw an awful trail of footprints, clear to him even in the darkness.

But now, as he looked across one more quadrangle, there was a huge tower, narrow and round. Boy could see the southern wall of the palace not far beyond; this had to be the South Tower. Suddenly he realized the futility of his situation.

He assumed that the doors were locked, but that he would be able to open them. Even given that he could get inside, he saw that he had little chance of finding Willow. The Old South Tower stretched away above him into the snowy night sky. He counted eight floors at least before he could make out no more. As he approached the tower, he saw that while it had looked narrow from a distance it was actually enormous. He stopped, and tried to decide what to do. In a situation like this, Valerian would have stopped, and turned to Boy. Boy could practically hear his voice.

"What do we need to do, Boy?" he would have asked. Even during those last few days, Valerian had always addressed Boy with the problem in hand logically, trying to get him to think logically too, about the solution. The force of habit had been instilled in him well.

But what could he do? He skirted round the tower as far as he was able. He estimated there could be at least six rooms on each floor. He tried hard to calculate how many rooms that made if there were even only eight floors, but gave up before he had the answer. It was useless.

He felt like screaming, shouting "Willow!" and just running before anyone could catch them, but he knew that was stupid. They'd be caught long before they found their way to the outside world. Yet something in him would not give up.

He was moving back around the base of the building toward a doorway, when he noticed something strange at his feet. The snow was darker here, and slushy underfoot. Glancing up, he saw a low archway to his right that led down beneath a building at the foot of the tower. The trail of tainted snow led into the archway. Without thinking what he was doing, Boy walked toward the low archway, and then he heard a noise. It sounded like whimpering, like a hurt animal, but there was something else too. A wet noise that Boy couldn't quite place.

Wishing he had brought the lamp with him, he stuck his head into the archway. The noise was more distinct.

He wondered if he should call out; if there was someone hurt they might need help. But he couldn't risk giving himself away. Even as he decided this, he thought of Willow, and felt bad. She would help, even if it meant risking her own safety.

He moved a little way into the tunnel and was about to call out when he sensed something else. A smell that immediately made him understand what was happening. The darkened, wet snow, the gurgling noise, the whimpering. The smell was blood.

Without being able to help himself, he let out a cry of fear. The noise stopped and a dark shape moved before him. It was a hulking figure, crouched over something twitching on the ground. As it turned, Boy looked straight into its face.

For a moment there was nothing. Boy took in too many horrors in an instant. The poor thing dead on the tunnel floor. The Phantom sitting on its prey, blood dripping from its mouth. And its eyes, worst of all, its eyes.

The thing looked at him, failing to react, staring at him. Then Boy screamed and ran from the tunnel, heedless that anyone might hear him or see him as he flailed his way back across the palace grounds.

It took him a long while to realize he was not being followed, but still he did not feel safe.

He kept on running the way he had come, his legs burning, a stitch in his side; he did not stop till he was back at the door from which he had emerged an hour or so before.

He slowed only briefly as he let himself back in, past the sleeping guard. He hurtled back up through his secret stairwell to his rooms, where he locked himself in, and stood shaking, his legs wobbling and his shoulders rising and falling. He climbed into bed fully clothed, and began to cry at the shock of what he had seen.

After a long time he grew tired of crying, and only dull aching pain remained. He tried to push the sight from his mind, but it was futile. He could not shift from his thoughts the image of the poor animal, or worse, person, who had died at the Phantom's hands. And the Phantom itself. Not that large in truth. A small figure, but powerfully built, especially around its shoulders and arms, it had crouched like one of the apes Boy had once seen in the traveling menageries that sometimes came to the City. And its face. Its face was too awful to tell, and its hair was thin and patchy, revealing large areas of scalp underneath. The eyes were the worst of it; there was something about the eyes that had scared Boy to within an inch of his life. They were almost totally blank eyes, with maybe nothing more behind them but the thought of killing, and yet that was not quite all. There was something else in those eyes that had burnt its way into Boy's mind and remained there now, yet Boy could not understand what it was.

Other thoughts rushed into his mind, not least the fear that he had left a trail that anyone or anything would be able to follow right back to the Winter Rooms, or at least to the entrance downstairs. He shivered, and longed for the snow to fall more thickly than ever, to hide his footprints, and to hide the blood, and to take all his pain away.

"Please snow, please snow, please snow," he repeated to himself, again and again.

Despite being fully clothed, despite the warmth of his room, and the thickness of his sheets, Boy trembled as he desperately longed for sleep to come and take him.

8

It was not only thoughts of the Phantom that kept Boy awake. There was Willow too. What if she was not safely locked up in the Tower? With that thing on the loose? But nowhere was really safe. He spent a wretched night, anticipating the commotion that would start at daybreak when the bloody mess was discovered.

But when morning dawned, there was nothing. The old blind servant came and went, bringing him his breakfast, and said nothing of murder.

As she was leaving, Boy stopped her.

"What is it, Boy?"

"I just wondered if you'd heard anything happening in the palace this morning. Anything strange . . . ?"

The woman shook her head.

"Same as ever," she said.

After she left, Boy moved to the window. There had indeed been much more snow overnight, and Boy prayed it was enough to hide everything that had happened.

From his high vantage point he could see a man with a shovel clearing some of the footpaths around the small square beneath his window. The snow was coming down, and Boy began to feel calmer, but Willow was still on his mind.

His thoughts were broken as the door to the outer room of his chambers burst open.

Maxim strode in and Boy could see he was not in a good mood.

Had he learnt of Boy's nocturnal activities, or was he furious about the murderous Phantom? But it seemed that no one knew Boy had escaped, and that no one knew, or cared, about whom the Phantom killed either inside the palace, or out.

"The girl was not there!" Maxim marched right up to Boy, who kept his nerve and didn't flinch. That seemed to throw Maxim, who for once did not lash out. Boy had had enough of threats and beatings. He had seen something far worse that night, and somehow the shock of it had given him a weird strength. What was a physical blow compared to what he'd seen in the tunnel?

"I could have told you that," Boy said, enjoying the irony of the situation. He knew exactly where "the girl" was, right here in the palace, while Maxim was scouring the City for her.

"How? Where is she?"

Under your very nose, Boy thought.

"I have no idea," he lied, "but I can tell you she's smarter than your guards. They won't find her."

Maxim pushed Boy back against a wall.

"Are you going to hurt me again?" Boy asked, flatly. He felt utterly calm.

Maxim was taken aback. The boy was in a strange mood, and he had no time for games.

"No," he said. "I'm not. But unless you tell me where the book is, I will send you somewhere where you will die. The dark flight? Remember that, Boy. Just remember that."

Boy no longer felt so strong. He scratched his nose, looking away from Maxim.

"Ah," said Maxim. "So you know what I'm talking about? Good. Then tell me this: Where is the book? If the girl has it, where is she? If not, who does have it? If you do not tell me now, I will have you taken straight away. . . ."

Boy edged away from the wall, and crossed to a window, to look at the snow. What could he say? Even if he told Maxim about Kepler, that he and Willow were in the palace, it still might not bring the book into his hands. Boy had no idea whether Kepler had it with him. It would have been a risk to bring it, it would have been a risk to leave it behind. And if he told Maxim all that, the one certain thing was that Willow would be in danger too. There was nothing he could say.

"I don't know," he said, so calmly and clearly that Maxim could do nothing other than believe him. Boy felt he had been living on borrowed time ever since New Year's Eve. Valerian had nearly killed him then. Had changed his mind at the last moment, or had it changed for him, by Kepler's telling him Boy was his son. Either Boy would have died, or his father. Now all Boy wanted was for Willow to be safe.

"Throw me to the Phantom, then, if you must. I can't tell you where the book is, because I don't know."

Boy expected Maxim to shout at him, to curse him, to beat him and to have him taken that very moment, but he did none of these things. He sat on a chair and shook his head.

Boy moved away from the window.

"Why?" he asked.

Maxim looked up.

"Why do you need the book? Why does the emperor need it? It was here once before, and nothing good came of it."

"The doctor told you that, didn't he? He had his uses, but you know, I thought he might have lost his mind. . . ."

"I think he very nearly did. What did he do to deserve that? What was it, to put him in prison for what . . . ? Ten years?"

"Fifteen," Maxim corrected him. "Fifteen. He knew too much. I couldn't allow that. I was the only other person left alive who knew what he knew."

"So why didn't you kill him?" Boy said bitterly. "You kill people so easily here."

Maxim looked at him wryly.

"Maybe not so easily in those days. But there was another reason. We needed his skills . . . as a doctor."

"Why?" asked Boy, interested to see whether Maxim would tell him about the Phantom, admit that they knew of its existence, that they even cared for it, and needed Bedrich to try to control it.

"You think I'm going to tell you all the secrets in this place, Boy? Don't be so stupid. I am only interested in you for one reason. The book. You were with Valerian at the end, you must know what happened to it."

Boy shook his head.

"The book was the last thing on our mind. Valerian was taken. Willow and I left the Yellow House. The Tower was a ruin. If your men didn't find it when they captured me then it must have been looted before I went back that day."

Maxim studied Boy's face, as if trying to ascertain the truth of his words.

"But why do you need it anyway?" Boy asked. "Why does the emperor need it?"

"Because he's mad!" Maxim spat, then paused. He sighed. "I need it to give the emperor the one thing he hasn't got. Life."

"What do you mean?" asked Boy. "He's alive now. . . ."

"You noticed? Hmm. But for how much longer? He's seventy-eight now, and, as you see, as frail as a man twenty years older. He's a puny, feeble, fake old man, and he wants to live forever."

"He wants to what?" spluttered Boy.

"He wants to live forever," Maxim said, as if it was the most reasonable thing in the world. "There is no one to succeed him. He is the last of a direct family line that stretches back for seven centuries at least. When he dies . . ."

"And so he wants to live forever, instead? He's mad!"

Maxim glanced at Boy, not very interested.

"I should have you killed for that. But yes, you're right.

Unfortunately for me, I have to find a way of making him immortal, before he gets tired of my failing to do so."

"I see," said Boy. "Or rather, I don't see. He wants to be made immortal. Say you find the book, say you find the book and find an answer. What then?"

Now Maxim did seem interested in what Boy was saying. "What do you mean?"

"Well, suppose the book tells you a magical thing to do to him, to make him live forever. A spell or whatever. You do this thing to the emperor, and he thinks he's immortal."

"What of it?"

"Well, how's he going to know any different unless he dies?"

There was a long silence, during which Maxim stared hard at Boy. The moment was broken by a knock at the door. The younger serving girl came in.

"Maxim, sir," she began.

"Not now!" Maxim shouted.

"But, sir, the emperor wants you. Right now, sir."

"Dammit!" Maxim said, rising from his chair. "Very well, I'm coming."

He turned to Boy.

"Don't go anywhere, will you?" he said, smiling. "You've reached the end of your usefulness. You will stay here until I think what to do with you."

Boy stood up.

"But, sir," the girl said to Maxim. "His Highness wants to see Boy, too. He says he's to attend court from now on."

Maxim swore and grabbed her by the arm.

"Are you sure?" he barked, but there was no reason to

suppose otherwise. He let her go, kicked a chair over and stormed from the room.

"Get here!" he yelled over his shoulder.

Boy skittered out the door after Maxim, marveling at how his life might just have been saved by the City's legendary, lunatic, decrepit emperor.

9

Willow. The first thing Boy saw on entering court, through the crowds of people, was Willow. She had spotted him immediately too, and smiled. Boy risked a smile back, while Maxim's attention was taken with hurrying over to the emperor, who was already sitting in his throne, awaiting them.

"So, Maxim, you have failed again!"

The emperor's weedy voice sailed over the hushed courtroom. The silence that followed was absolute.

Boy could sense the tension in the room. Even during his short time there he had learnt what a perilous existence they all led, living on the emperor's whims. Maxim was no exception.

"Well, Maxim, what do you have to say?"

Boy took his chance.

He had lagged behind Maxim, on whom the whole attention of the court was now focused. Ever so slowly, trying to think himself as small and unnoticeable as possible, Boy sidestepped toward Willow and Kepler. No one seemed to notice; all eyes in the room were fixed on the scene playing out between Frederick and Maxim.

"Well! You have failed to find the book! What exactly do you intend to do now?"

Maxim took a step forward and seemed to be about to speak, but Frederick was working himself up into a rage.

"I charge you with one simple duty, and you consistently fail to deliver your promises! I swear you are doing it deliberately! You want me to die, do you? Do you? Well, you'll be gone long before me, Maxim. I've had enough! I've had enough of your pathetic excuses, and it won't be allowed to continue!"

Boy had made it to Willow's side.

He brushed the back of her hand with his, but could think of nothing to say.

"Boy," Willow said.

Kepler turned and saw who it was.

He smiled, then frowned. He glared at Boy.

"You mustn't be seen with us," he hissed. "It's dangerous."

"You don't understand," Boy whispered back. "It's more dangerous here than you know."

"What do you mean?" Willow asked.

Boy was about to answer, but one of the ladies standing nearby was looking at them. Boy turned away from Willow and pretended to watch the scene unfolding in front of them. After a while he spoke to Willow without looking at her, keeping his eyes on Frederick and Maxim.

"It's dangerous. Those two for a start," he whispered, and nodded slightly toward the dais. "But there's something else. The Phantom. The Phantom lives here, under the palace."

Boy risked looking round at Willow. Her face was a picture of confusion. Boy looked forward again.

"Later," he whispered so quietly that only she could hear. "Meet me here tonight."

Finally Maxim managed to speak.

"Sire, I wonder how you came across the news that I do not have the book?"

"From the captain of the Imperial Guard."

"But my men—"

"*Your* men, Maxim? *Your* men? The Imperial Guard are mine. They do not serve you! They serve me! You forget your place. The Imperial Guard exist to serve me, and earlier today I spoke to their captain, who tells me that the book was not found on their expedition across the City!"

Frederick was so angry that he might do anything.

"But, sire," Maxim said calmly, "we do have the book."

He stopped to emphasize his words.

"What?" said Frederick, crisply.

Boy and Willow were transfixed.

"We *do* have the book," Maxim continued. "It *was* found on the mission to the City. Even now it is in my chambers. I was on my way here to bring you this great news. I will begin consultation immediately, after I have . . . spoken to the captain of the Guard."

Boy turned to Willow, who shook her head ever so slightly. Of course he didn't have the book, so what game was he playing at? Whatever it was, Boy knew the stakes were being raised ever higher with each passing moment.

"When can I see it?" Frederick asked deliberately.

"But, sire, I thought it best if it remained safe with me," Maxim said cautiously. He approached the dais, and whispered.

"After what happened . . . before, it might be best to keep it hidden. . . ."

Frederick's face was a horrible picture. Memories contorted his features into anguish. The look froze on his face, briefly; then he shook himself.

"Yes," he said, feebly. "Yes. You're right."

Maxim stood upright again and spoke brightly.

"Is it not wonderful news? At last our goal is in sight."

Frederick nodded, looking like a child in his huge throne.

"Yes" was all he said.

"I shall ensconce myself in my rooms. I will devote all hours of day and night to this endeavor. I will consult and scry and when I have an answer from the book we will prepare to make you . . . immortal!"

He finished with a flourish so extravagant that the whole court burst into applause without even really wanting to.

Frederick sat on his throne, his mouth twitching slightly, as he tried and failed to regain his composure, though no one noticed.

While people were talking and clapping, Boy leant in to Willow so that only she could hear him.

"Are you locked in?"

Willow shook her head.

"Good, then tonight. After midnight."

Kepler grabbed Willow's arm and began to pull her away. She was about to protest when she saw that Maxim was striding toward Boy. The court was over and people were starting to leave. Maxim came up to Boy and glanced at Willow and Kepler. He seemed to be about to say something.

"Are we going now?" Boy said quickly to Maxim, trying to show no interest in Willow or Kepler. "Can I help you?"

Maxim was still looking at Willow, a question on his lips, but now he turned to Boy.

"Help me? Help me!" he snorted. He grabbed Boy and began to walk him out of the court. Boy dared not risk a look back at Willow.

"Of course you can't help me. But unfortunately, Emperor Frederick thinks you are useful, so you will come with me for the time being. When I have made him immortal, however, it will be a different story."

They had left the room now and were heading back upstairs.

"What?" Boy asked. "What will happen to me then?"

Maxim didn't break step.

"You will have outlived your usefulness. You and all those tricksters and charlatans who hang around him like flies on a carcass."

"But you don't even have the book!" Boy cried.

That did make Maxim stop. He slapped his hand over Boy's mouth and pushed him against a wall.

"Do you want everyone in the palace to hear?" he snapped. "Keep that to yourself, or I'll finish you now, and tell Frederick you had an accident."

He held his hand on Boy's mouth, until a serving girl appeared at one end of the corridor. He let Boy go and pulled him into a walk again.

"So be careful," he said. "Be careful what you say. Anyway, you won't have a chance to speak to anyone else. You can stay in your room until I'm ready for you."

"But how are you going to make him immortal? You don't have the book."

They were at the doors to Boy's chamber.

Maxim pushed him inside and closed the door behind them, so the guard outside could not hear.

"No!" he said. "I don't have the book. And I don't need it either."

He turned to leave, and opened the door again.

"I don't understand," Boy said.

"Really? You should. It was you who provided the solution. I can't believe I didn't think of it myself. I have been too absorbed by it all, maybe. It doesn't matter now. You will excuse me. I have to visit the captain of the Guard. I think it's time he was replaced."

10

Night in the palace.

Different worlds enacted themselves in different parts of the palace, but it would have been a mistake to suppose these worlds were entirely isolated from each other, for they were all part of a single, if intricate, dance.

In the Royal Bedchambers, Frederick snored gently, muttering in his sleep, through which pleasant dreams of his coming immortality wrestled with nightmares of less pleasant things, things from the past that he had thought were forgotten. He wore a red nightcap, whose long red tassel dangled across his face, looking in the half-light like a trail of dried blood.

He turned in his sleep, calling out from time to time, but not waking. The guards at his door ignored it all, being well used to the emperor's ways.

Nearby in the adjacent wing of the palace, the emperor's right hand, confidante, doctor, servant, advisor and counselor, Maxim, paced around his study. Finally he sat down in a velvet armchair by the fire, and scratched his bald head. He was weighing up certain matters. He had an answer for Frederick now. He had a solution. If it worked, then all would be well, and Maxim would be safe. If it failed, then the irritable old fool might have him sent down that dreadful stairway. But he had decided one thing, and that was that to fail to act at all would probably be fatal anyway. Frederick was getting more erratic with each day that passed. Maxim knew he was living on borrowed time, and that he had stalled as much as he was able to. He had to do something now.

Idly he threw more coals onto the fire, and as he did so, thoughts flowed into his head. What a strange life it had been! He didn't want it to end now, but there had been so much death, so much killing, and now that he was older, and maybe a little wiser, he saw it as a disease. Death had been all around him for so long, and he felt in very real danger of catching the dying disease himself.

When he'd been in the dungeons he'd heard Bedrich singing that song, the song from so long ago, written by Sophia Beebe. Since he'd heard it again he hadn't been able to shift it from his mind for very long. It seemed so apt at the moment; maybe that was why all these thoughts of the past were coming back to him now, all these thoughts of death.

Had she even used the book herself? Foreseen her own future, and that of everyone else tied up in its demonic designs? It was an appalling thought, one that made him feel powerless. Still the tune ran through his head, and he hummed to himself.

> *Surely you won't run,*
> *When your boat is ready to sail.*
> *Surely you will stand*
> *And face the gentle rain?*

In the morning you should think
You might not last unto the night,
In the evening you should think
You might not last unto the morn.
So dance, my dears, dance,
Before you take the dark flight down.

Maxim stopped humming and bitterly spat into the fire. He was far from ready to take the journey, the long dark journey to oblivion. He would beat the emperor at his own game yet, and do away with all the hangers-on who made his life so much more complicated than it need be. If it was just him and the emperor, he could control things. One way or the other, it would be over soon.

And then there was Boy, who once again sat by the darkening window watching the snow unbelievably still falling from the clouded heavens, hiding all trace of dirt and grime from view. He waited until it was dark and then waited some more. Someone brought him his supper, and he ate it gratefully enough. He reflected grimly that he was eating better than he ever had in his life, and yet he wanted nothing more than to escape.

Escape.

It was the only thing to do. Find Willow and escape. Kepler could look after himself as far as Boy was concerned.

Boy waited all through the dark evening, after his tray had been taken away, waited and waited for each tolling of the City and palace bells, until midnight came. As he waited he inevitably started to think about Valerian. Valerian, his father. No, he didn't know that for sure, but he felt it. At least, he felt there was something in the way Kepler had tried to conceal what he had spoken, that told him it was the truth. And what then? If he had lived with his father all those years, being bullied and tormented, and not even realized it? Did that bring him peace? It might not tell him everything, and he might never know who his mother was, but it would be a start. At least then he would know something about himself, in the way other people did.

The midnight bells struck softly through the snow-laden night. Once again Boy made his way with his lockpick down the secret stairwell, but this time headed for the court itself. He knew his way around a few parts of the palace quite well now, from his rooms to the court, but nonetheless he felt on unknown ground as he approached the huge chamber. By night, and with no one else around, it was a very different place. During the day, it was full of color and life and people and wealth. By night, it was a different thing. The place seemed even bigger when empty, and the colors muted. It was a deserted, forgotten place. Haunted.

Boy stole across the marble ocean of the floor, and was happier when his footfalls landed on thick carpets instead. He tried to decide where to wait for Willow, and spotted a corner by the side of the fireplace that would be perfect. He was making for it when Willow stepped from the shadows.

"Boy!" she cried, and rushed to him.

They held each other for a long time before either of them spoke again.

Finally they pulled apart, and looked at each other.

There were too many questions. Too many words that needed to be spoken.

"How are you?"

"What happened? You didn't come. . . ."

"I know. I'm sorry. I was captured. There was no way to tell you. . . ."

Willow held Boy's hands. They moved and sat down next to each other on the dais, just in front of the throne. Two small figures dwarfed by the vastness of the darkened courtroom.

"What did you mean about the Phantom?" Willow asked.

"Just what I said!" Boy said. "It lives in the palace, under it really. I was kept in the dungeons, and there's a flight of stairs that leads down to somewhere even deeper. That's where it lives, then comes out to . . ."

Boy stopped. He didn't want to think about it.

"And they don't know about it?"

"Oh yes, they do. Well, Maxim does, at least. They seem to tolerate it, as long as it doesn't murder in the palace itself."

"Don't worry," Willow said, seeing Boy was upset by it. "We're together again, now."

"But what did you think when I didn't meet you by the fountain?"

"I knew. I knew you wouldn't just leave me. But I was so worried."

"How did you know I was here?"

"A feather. They left a white feather behind in the house. Kepler said it was the Imperial Guard."

"He was right. I should thank him for that, at least."

Willow shrugged.

"I don't like him. I suppose he's trying to help, but I really don't like him."

"He's come here to get me back, I suppose?"

Willow nodded.

"I don't understand," Boy said. "I know he thinks I belong to him now that Valerian's gone, but you wouldn't think he'd risk his life to get me, would you?"

"Never mind," Willow said. "We can forget him. Boy, let's just get out of here and start again, as we meant to."

"Yes," said Boy. "Yes."

"There is one thing, though. I don't know if there's a good time to tell you, so I think I should tell you now."

"What?" Boy asked, wondering why he suddenly felt scared.

Willow hesitated.

"What?" Boy asked. "Tell me!"

"Boy. It's about Valerian. He's not your father."

Boy said nothing, but flinched as if he had been struck.

"No," he said. "That's not true. No. You can't know that."

"Boy," said Willow gently. "It's true. I found out from Kepler."

"He told you?"

"Not exactly. We were talking about you. Well, arguing really. I told him he'd been terrible to you, to split us up, to send you back to the Yellow House, and only a few days after you'd seen your father die."

"What did he say?"

"He shouted at me that your father wasn't dead. He said he only told Valerian that to make you live."

Boy said nothing now, but just sat, slowly shaking his head.

"He gambled that Valerian would believe him, that there was one small bit of Valerian that wanted to believe he had a son, and could not kill that son for his own sake.

"Valerian told us he made the pact to spend one night with the woman he desired. And he did, but somehow in the morning she still rejected him.

"Kepler told me something, something I'd already suspected. He loved that woman too. She was called Helene. That was why he and Valerian fell out, became enemies when they had been friends before. Neither of them saw Helene again, but Kepler knew he could use that story to make Valerian believe you were his son, even just for a short while. Long enough, in fact, for him to go to his death, instead of you to yours. But he's not your father. He's not."

"Then who is?" Boy cried. "Who is?"

"I don't know," Willow said. "Kepler wouldn't say, and when I pushed him for an answer, he got angry and sent me to bed."

She stopped, trying to think of what she could say to Boy, who sat with his head hanging in his hands, but finding no words that could help.

"I'm sorry" was all she said, in the end. "Let's get away from here, at least, shall we? There'll be time later to think."

Boy looked up at her.

"No," he said.

"What do you mean?" Willow asked.

"I mean, no. I'm not going anywhere. Not until I have

some answers. I don't want to think about things later. I want some answers now."

Willow put her hand on Boy's arm, but he did not take it. He stood and looked down at her. She had never seen him like this before.

"I've had enough, Willow," he said. "I've had enough of not knowing who I am, who my parents were, where I was born. I don't even have a name!"

"Yes, you do, you're Boy, you told me that. . . ."

"I don't care what I told you! I want a proper name, I want to know who I am! I'm not going anywhere until I get some answers."

"Please, Boy, let's go. Let's get out of this bad place first and then think about it later. Please?"

"No," said Boy. "No. I'm staying here."

"But what good will that do?"

"The book," said Boy. "The book is here, isn't it? Maxim may think he's just pretending it is, but it is here. Kepler has it, doesn't he?"

Willow looked at the floor.

"Yes, I think he does," she said quietly.

"Then I'm going to look in it."

"No!" Willow said, gripping his arm tightly. "You know how dangerous it can be! You mustn't."

"I don't care how dangerous it is. Haven't you been listening to me at all? I want to know the truth about myself now, no matter what the risk. I have to know!"

Willow shook her head.

"But we can't even get to it. I think it's in the bag he brought with him. It's very heavy and I've seen precious

186

little else come out of there. But he never leaves me alone, we'd never get the chance to see."

"Then we'll make a chance," said Boy. "That's all there is to it."

Willow stared at Boy. There was something new about him, something stronger than she had ever seen before.

"The only question," Boy said, "is will you help me?"

Willow stood and held Boy's hands for a long time. She smiled, gazing into his eyes.

"Of course I'll help you. We're together now, see?"

Boy smiled, and leant toward Willow. He kissed her and smiled, then looked more serious again, the air of strength returning to him.

"Listen to me, then," he said. "We don't have much time. Maxim's about to make his move, and when he does, he'll kill us all. You, me, Kepler. All the alchemists and astrologers. No one will be safe once Frederick's immortal. Tomorrow, we will be in court. Kepler will be called too. And we'll make a chance to look at the book. I'm fighting now, Willow. I've been pushed around enough and I'm going to put an end to it."

Willow smiled and nodded. She only wished she felt as sure as Boy seemed to be.

11

Boy was right. Maxim was ready to make his move. When Boy woke next morning he found the young serving girl already in his room.

"What is it? What's going on?"

Boy got down out of bed and scratched his nose.

"Today's the day!" the girl declared.

"What are you talking about?"

"The emperor. Maxim's going to make him immortal today. This evening, in court."

Boy almost felt like laughing.

"Don't you understand?" he asked as he got dressed. "Don't you understand anything about this place? What do you think will happen once Frederick's immortal?"

"What?" asked the girl, surprised.

"No one will be safe. Maxim will see to that. And Frederick will just go on getting madder and madder with no end to it all."

The girl ignored him, and began to tidy things in the room. Boy gave up.

"There's one person who's not invited," she said, not smiling for once. "You."

Boy raised an eyebrow.

"Maxim says you're to remain here."

Boy smiled. It might work in his favor. Maybe he could get to the book while everyone else was occupied in court.

He crossed to the window and scowled at the falling snow. He had had enough of it. He had believed it was going to help him, he had trusted it to hide all the horror away, but it had failed. He cursed it, and himself for being so stupid as to think it could save him. He was going to have to save himself.

12

The whole palace was astir. The news had spread from the highest bell tower to the lowest cellar. Everyone was talking about the emperor's immortality.

There was a huge uproar in the Old South Tower. Frederick's astrologers and other advisors were shocked at the news. Willow and Kepler listened to the debates over the communal breakfast they took in the tower refectory. There was disagreement over what it would mean, and over exactly what Maxim was going to do, and much, much argument about the book, and about whether it even existed, never mind whether Maxim had it.

Kepler stared at the plate in front of him. He and Willow were the only people in the room not discussing the forthcoming events.

"Don't be so obvious," she hissed.

Kepler looked up and saw what she meant.

"Let's go back to our rooms," he said.

"What do you think Maxim's going to do?" Willow asked, as they walked up the spiral staircase.

"Just what he says, probably."

"But he doesn't have the book," Willow said. "You have it, don't you?"

"Be quiet!" They had reached their rooms, at the very top of the tower, and Kepler flung the door shut behind them.

"Yes, I do have the book, and if anyone finds that out, we're as good as dead. Just to own it means death! People will kill to own it. So keep quiet."

He stormed off across the room.

"But why did you bring it?"

"I couldn't take the risk of leaving it anywhere. Nowhere is safe. They'd ransacked the Yellow House looking for it. If they made a connection from Valerian to me, as they undoubtedly will sooner or later, they'd have gone looking for it at my house too. The only safe place is where I can keep an eye on it."

"But what are we going to do?" she asked. She knew full well what her plans with Boy were, but what if Kepler's own plans got in the way?

"I don't know. It's turned out differently from what I planned. And once Maxim does his performance today . . ."

"You mean you got us in here with no idea about getting us out again?"

"Getting in was the hard part, but that's not what I mean. And if I can get things back to what I had planned, we won't need to worry about getting out again."

"What are you talking about?" Willow asked.

"Enough. You'll see later. Now tell me what you and Boy spoke about yesterday."

"No!" said Willow. "I want to know what you mean. Why won't we need to worry about getting out?"

"I said enough! What did you and Boy speak about at court?"

"You expect me to tell you, but you won't trust me with your plans? You can think again!"

Kepler grunted and strode to the window, where he gazed out at the City far below.

Willow watched him; then her eyes were drawn to the large leather bag lying under Kepler's bed. Its mouth lay slightly open, and though she couldn't be sure, Willow thought she could see the corner of a book poking out. A huge, weighty tome. The book from the Dead Days when Valerian had died.

And now Boy wanted to look inside it. Her heart began to race.

13

Boy had spent the day idly, locked up in his luxurious prison, and dusk had fallen. The ceremony was due to start in court soon, and he had been prepared to wait for a good moment to sneak out and down to the tower.

To the tower, to find the book, and then . . .

Then to know who and what he really was. If Valerian was not his father, then who? Kepler must know; he'd looked in the book enough by now to know all about Boy, surely, assuming that that was what he was looking for. But Kepler did seem to have become obsessed by Boy, by possessing him as Valerian had. Boy couldn't believe Kepler didn't have all the answers.

And Valerian? Boy thought deeply about his former master, and despite all the hurt and pain he'd inflicted, Boy could find nothing in his heart now for Valerian, nothing but sorrow. Sorrow that he had died, that they had failed to make things better between them, but more than these regrets was a greater sorrow.

That Valerian wasn't his father after all.

Maxim might not have wanted Boy to be present during the ceremony, but Frederick had had other ideas, and once again had ordered that his new plaything be brought to court.

A guard walked Boy down through the palace, to find Maxim himself waiting outside the door to the court. He dismissed the guard, and watched him go.

"You will say nothing unless I tell you to," Maxim threatened. Boy acted suitably cowed. It wouldn't hurt for Maxim to think he was too scared to act.

"The old fool wants you here, you're his favorite new pet, and there's nothing I can do about that. Not yet. So behave yourself."

Boy nodded.

Maxim opened the door and they entered.

Yet again the palace outshone its own magnificence. The room had been decorated with flags and banners; strips of red and gold silk hung all around, encrusted with jewels that sparkled in the light from four massive chandeliers hanging from the painted ceiling. The room was packed. Far more so than usual. Boy looked around for Willow, but could not see her, or Kepler.

There was standing room only, and precious little of that. Boy marveled at the accumulation of wealth upon each person present. Even the lowliest members of the palace were dressed in fine clothes, maybe only brought out on occasions of the greatest importance. And there could be no occasion more important than this.

The Bestowing of Immortality on Emperor Frederick.

A fanfare rang out across the room, and the emperor was carried in on a large chair slung between two poles, festooned with more ribbons of red and gold, supported by four men. The people struggled to allow him by, and it took some time for the small cortege to make its way to the dais.

Once there, Frederick climbed up onto his throne as usual, and turned to face the assembly. He smiled, and Boy almost felt sorry for him, but was then horrified to see the emperor looking straight at him.

"Boy! There you are. Come here! You must be here."

Boy hesitated, and looked at Maxim, who inclined his head slowly.

"Yes, you must be here," Frederick drawled. "You are a good and faithful servant to the empire. If more of these idiots acted with your quick thinking maybe it wouldn't have taken so long to get to where we are today. . . ."

Maxim and Boy stood at the foot of the dais. Frederick looked around once more, and coughed.

"People," he said, in his wavering voice, "today is a great day. Thanks to my hard work and struggles, I will today achieve a wonderful thing. I am an old man; there is no . . . heir . . . to the throne. But this problem will be a problem no longer. I have created a superb solution. It will make everything well. You will not be deprived of your beloved emperor after my death, for I am not going to die. In a few moments I will have Maxim do . . . whatever it is he must do . . . and I will become immortal!"

There was a gasp and then a murmur around the court room. Even though everyone knew already that this was what the old emperor had been seeking, it was still a shock to actually hear him say it.

Frederick frowned at Maxim.

"Why don't they cheer?" he asked.

"They're just too happy to express what they really feel,

sire," Maxim said, and he nodded to a guard. Boy watched as the guard pulled his sword an inch or two from its scabbard and glared at some people near to him. They immediately started to clap, and as others began to applaud and cheer, the emperor sat back on his throne, satisfied.

Maxim chewed his lip, and ran one hand across the top of his bald head. He let the cheering continue for a full minute or two. It would be a good idea, he thought, to put the emperor in as good a mood as possible. Finally he raised his hand.

"Loyal servants of the Imperial Throne, lords, ladies, dukes, duchesses, marquises. Behold! For today is the first day of a new chapter in the history of the empire, and you are its witnesses.

"I have obtained knowledge that was occult, but is no longer hidden, for it has fallen into my hands, knowledge that will free our emperor from the constraints of mortality. Having made certain careful preparations, I am about to perform the ritual that will bestow everlasting life on Emperor Frederick the Magnificent!"

He paused, and after a moment, a subdued cheer came from the crowd.

"Of course," Maxim continued, "this ritual is delicate and powerful in equal measure. It cannot be witnessed directly. We will begin at once."

He nodded once more to two of the guards standing near the throne.

"The screen!" he cried.

A large screen made of a wooden frame over which red silk had been stretched was placed round the three forward sides of the dais, so that Frederick was hidden.

As he disappeared from sight, the emperor still wore a silly smile. He lifted a hand to his people, and then was gone. Boy stood by the dais, staring at Maxim, who clapped his hands. From the back of the hall, another servant brought forward a tray, on which were certain objects. Magical devices, no doubt, but nothing that Boy thought could bestow immortality. A wand, a cup, a potion and some herbs were all Boy could see as the things were taken up the steps of the dais and behind the screen. Suddenly, as Boy watched Maxim, he was reminded of something. He had a feeling that he had seen all this before. He'd described it to Valerian once, who had told him it had a French name, déjà vu. Already seen, Valerian had said. That was just what Boy felt as he watched Maxim, but this déjà vu had a mundane explanation. Boy had seen this countless times, onstage, with Valerian. A flowery speech, a few props, a screen. It was all exactly as Valerian had done it, pulling some illusion or other, and fooling a whole crowd into believing something impossible.

What was Maxim up to?

He stepped to the front of the dais once more, exactly like Valerian stepping to the front of the stage to make sure he had the audience's attention before performing the trick.

"Behold!" he cried. "In a few moments, your emperor will be immortal!"

And he whipped behind the screen.

A murmur spread round the room, so that Boy could not hear anything that was going on behind the screen, but from where he stood, Boy could see vague shapes moving behind it. Maybe Maxim had intended it, maybe not, but the light from lamps on the wall behind the dais was casting the shadows of Maxim and Frederick onto the silk of the screen.

Others had noticed this too. Boy saw Maxim pick up the cup. He handed it to Frederick, who put it to his lips.

Boy's heart jumped. That was it! Maxim was simply going to poison Frederick. Right there, in front of everyone, he was going to poison him, and then claim he had died in the arduous process of achieving immortality.

Boy moved, but a guard barred his way. Frederick drank from the cup. He waited for a scream of pain, or for Frederick to collapse to the floor. Nothing happened. The emperor gave the cup back to Maxim, who set it down.

Shapes moved, but Boy could see nothing of Frederick now. Maxim came and went around the throne, waving his hands in front of it, picking up other things from the tray, putting them down again. Finally, even Maxim's movements ceased. There was nothing, nothing at all. The muttering in court grew louder and louder.

The guard holding Boy was now so fascinated by what was going on that he let go, and moved closer to the screen. He took another step. He was just about to put his head around the back of it when it flew forward and clattered down the steps. Maxim stood with arms raised.

"Behold!" he cried. "Emperor Frederick is now immortal!"

There was a stunned silence, and then the cheering and shouting and clapping began. The emperor sat on his throne, as he had before. He was alive, but there was something not quite right about him. He still had a foolish grin on his face, but his eyes seemed to be drifting all around the room, roaming unfocused from floor to ceiling.

Boy looked at the cup, now on its side and empty of whatever it had contained, and then looked at the emperor again. What had Maxim given him?

People began to press forward, watching as the emperor moved not a muscle. The astrologers and alchemists peered at him closely. Maxim stepped in front of one of them who was getting a little closer than the others.

"What's wrong with him?" someone said.

"Nothing!" Maxim said. "Nothing. The process is an exhausting one. It will take a short while for the effects to wear off, and then . . . yes! See! Already His Highness is restored to himself! But no, it is more than that. For he is now immortal!"

The emperor stood. This perfectly normal action produced a gasp from the crowd, who all drew back.

"Is it done?" he said to Maxim. "Am I immortal now?"

There was something wrong with his voice, something Boy couldn't place, as if he was talking in a dream.

"Oh yes!" Maxim said. "You are now immortal. And since that is the case, I trust Your Highness will no longer see the need for the presence of certain people in court . . . ?"

Boy looked around. He could see guards moving around the walls of the court, making for where he and the astrologers stood. Finally he saw Willow and Kepler, standing with the other advisors.

Frederick nodded.

"I am immortal," he said, as much to himself as anyone else. He spoke more normally.

"Immortal," Maxim repeated. "So there is no need for these useless diviners anymore?"

Boy understood now. He saw the whole thing, and understood what Maxim had meant when he said that it was *he* who had provided the solution. A very final one for some.

"No!" he cried, jumping forward. "No! It's a trick!"

A guard grabbed him and threw him to the floor.

He wrestled free and ran to the dais, where he jumped onto the steps.

"It's a trick! It's a trick!"

Maxim made for him, as did two more guards, but Frederick stepped between them and Boy.

"Stay!" he cried. The guards hesitated, but Maxim did not.

He caught Boy and put out his hand to one of the guards.

"Quick! Give me your sword."

"Do nothing!" Frederick shrieked at the guard, who remained where he was.

"And you, Maxim, will wait, too, until we hear what Boy has to say. He was faithful to us once, we will hear what he has to say. If it is false, he will die, but I shall be the judge! I am the immortal emperor, and I shall be heard!"

Maxim stopped.

"You cannot take the words of this boy above me! I have given you the greatest—"

"*Silence!*" Frederick screamed so loudly that Maxim jumped. "Now, Boy, what do you have to say? And be very careful *what* you say."

Boy got up from the floor and edged away from Maxim.

200

He looked around the court, saw Willow and the fear on her face and felt himself grow stronger.

He pointed at Maxim.

"It's a trick! He hasn't made you immortal. He hasn't done anything to you, except maybe drugged you for ten minutes! He's bluffing."

"What do you mean?"

Maxim took a step toward Boy, his face full of menace. Boy stepped back.

"I gave the idea to him."

"What idea?"

"About being immortal. I said to him, how do you know you're immortal until you die?"

There was total silence.

"I . . . what?" asked Frederick. "I . . ."

"It's very simple," Boy said. "How do you know you're immortal now? Unless you die? Are you willing to try to find out? He's trying to trick you, because there's no other way to know."

Now people understood, and the emperor too.

He turned to Maxim.

"Is this true?"

Maxim fought to stay calm. Boy knew he would give himself away if he lost his head now.

"Of course not! The brat lies! Have him taken away and slaughtered at once."

He made a signal to a guard, but again Frederick stopped him.

"The next man who obeys anyone else's orders will die. You all listen to me, not Maxim! Now, Maxim, why do you say the boy is lying?"

"Because he's a lying urchin. You can't—"

"He doesn't even have the book!" Boy cried. "Ask him to show you the book!"

Maxim's face was swollen with rage, but still he managed to speak calmly.

"There's no need to have the book. It's too powerful to bring down here—"

Frederick stopped him.

"Bring me the book, Maxim."

Maxim was utterly motionless.

"Bring me the book, now, or you will die."

"No!" Maxim screamed. "I don't have the cursed book! And you aren't immortal! How could you be? It's impossible!"

Frederick recoiled as if he had been struck.

"Traitor!" he screamed.

"You stupid fool! Did you really think I could make you immortal?"

Maxim laughed bitterly, flung his hand out at the crowd.

"Look at them! They've all been waiting for you to die for years! And why? Because you don't have an heir! So you wanted to be immortal instead. Well, you're a bigger fool than I ever thought! And a liar, too. You do have an heir, don't you, Frederick? Why don't you tell everyone all about it?"

"Guards!" Frederick yelled. "Arrest him!"

Maxim laughed, and backed away around the side of the throne. Then he darted behind the massive chair. He flicked something in the wall and a secret door opened. He disappeared and the door shut behind him.

A guard ran over and tried to find the catch Maxim had used.

"It's locked from the inside," he said.

Frederick practically jumped onto his throne, and stood there, quivering with rage.

"Find him! Search the palace. Close all exits! Bring him to me!"

The Tower

The Place of Revelation

1

The whole court was in turmoil.

Guards raced here and there, as Frederick shouted orders from atop his throne.

Willow ran to Boy. Kepler hurried after her, pushing his way through the crowds, but Willow was faster and more nimble.

"Quick!" she said to Boy. "Now's our chance."

"Kepler's after us!"

"He can't follow both of us. Split up. I'll meet you in the South Tower. You know the way?"

Boy nodded.

"Go!" he cried, and pushed Willow away from him. She skittered toward the nearest door, just as Kepler got to Boy.

"Got you!" he said. "You're coming with me. I need you."

Boy wriggled free. Amid all the chaos, no one was paying them any attention.

"No!" Boy cried. "I don't want to."

"But it's not safe for you here!" Kepler shouted.

"I know that!" Boy laughed. "It's not safe for anyone here."

"You don't understand," Kepler said. "You're mine. You're all I need."

"Get away from me!" Boy cried.

He turned and began to push his way through the crowd. Kepler pursued, trying to get past people, but he could not keep up with Boy, who was used to moving his small frame through tight places. Boy was about halfway across the room, making for another door, when the noise in the court suddenly increased tenfold.

There were screams from the door, and a huge swell of people pushed back from the main entrance. Boy could see ladies being crushed in the panic, men screaming to get away, as a circle opened in the crowds.

There was Maxim, advancing on Frederick, who was still dancing about madly on the throne. But Maxim was not alone. He had brought someone, or rather something, with him. He held a chain of iron links in his hand, at the far end of which was a struggling, snarling, spitting creature.

The Phantom.

It could be nothing else but the creature Boy had met in the tunnel, squatting over its victim in the trampled snow.

Screams flew to the heaven-painted ceiling; some of the courtiers fainted on the spot, as the Phantom was led against its will through the shiny bright court. It scrabbled on the polished floor, fighting to keep on its feet, which were callused and strong. It loped on its hands, moving like an ape, though Boy could see it really was human, in an appalling, twisted way. It pulled against its chain, trying to get away from the bright world into which it had been dragged, but Maxim was a powerful man, and headed un-erringly for Frederick.

No one else in the room moved. Boy looked at the emperor. There was horror, anger, fear, disgust and repulsion on his face, but strangely, no surprise.

"So!" Maxim shouted.

He reached the foot of the dais, and turned and yanked so hard on the Phantom's chain that it lost its footing entirely and went skidding onto the floor, where it tried and failed at first to find its feet.

"So! Beautiful people!"

The room fell silent, everyone staring openmouthed at the creature struggling at Maxim's feet.

"So! There is your emperor. Frederick the Magnificent! Frederick who wished to be made immortal because he had no heir, no son to succeed him! But he lies!

"He lies! For there is a story to tell. Fifteen years ago, he took a consort. Sophia Beebe! And the book prophesied that there would be an heir. That much some of you know. You may remember that the Beebes were disgraced, and you may believe that the offspring died! But you were lied to!

"You want a son, Frederick? Well, here's your son! This killing thing, kept hidden from everyone for fifteen years. Your son, Frederick! Your son, this beast!"

Frederick stood on his throne, stricken with horror. He glanced from the Phantom to his people, who began to call out in fear and shame at what they were witnessing.

The Phantom had got to its feet, and squatted, crouching, spitting and struggling on its short chain. Boy could not take his eyes off it. There was something offensive, yet fascinating, about it. It was only a child really, but malformed and powerful beyond its years.

"No," Frederick said, quietly, weakly. "No, it—"

"Don't lie!" Maxim shouted. "You know it as well as I do, as well as Bedrich did! The only other witness from those days! You wanted an heir? Well, this is the rightful heir to the throne."

"Guards!" Frederick screamed. "Arrest him! Arrest him! And take that . . . thing . . . away!"

Maxim snarled as three guards closed in on him. Swiftly he moved close to the beast and loosed the chain from its neck. Maxim began to back off and one of the guards made for him.

Faster than Boy imagined possible, the Phantom, who thought it was being attacked, leapt at the guard, and clawed him away in a second. Blood welled across the polished floor, and people screamed. The chaos that had been stilled while Maxim made his speech returned in a moment. There was pushing and shouting; another guard tried to swing his sword at the Phantom, who jumped right over the blade, dispatching his assailant with ease as he landed on his feet again.

Maxim ran. The Phantom, maddened by fury and fear, lashed out at anyone who came near.

Boy joined others running from the room, but stumbled, and went sprawling over several other people. Kepler was nowhere to be seen, but the panic was universal. The furor continued behind them, as the beast became frenzied, lunging at people. Boy got to his feet, and saw that he was bleeding. He had fallen on the sword of one of the guards, which was so sharp he hadn't felt anything at first. He now bled from a gash in his right forearm. He grabbed it with his other hand and ran for his life.

He had to get to the South Tower and find Willow.

He made it through the door, and tried to work out which way to go, as the screaming continued in the court. Frederick was jumping up and down on his throne, ranting, but could no longer be heard.

The Phantom, still on the loose, saw a gap in the crowd, and loped toward the door. No one tried to get near it, to stop it. A dozen guards who had attempted to do so lay on the floor, badly injured.

As it emerged from the court, it saw something it liked. Blood. A trail of blood leading out across the marble floor of the hall.

It followed.

2

Boy ran as fast as he could, leaving the screams behind him. He hurried through the palace, through bits he knew, then bits he didn't, trying frantically to remember Willow's description of the interior route to the Old South Tower.

He passed no one. It seemed that the entire palace had been present for the bestowing of Frederick's immortality, and everyone had witnessed the farce it had become. Likewise, everyone had seen the horror of the Phantom—everyone except Willow. Boy quickened his pace, but he had to remember what she had said, and it would be worse to get lost altogether.

He came to a junction and couldn't remember Willow's instructions. He hesitated, then guessed left. Years of navigating the City's mazelike streets had given him a good sense of direction, and he decided to trust it now.

He was right. As he ran down a long corridor with tall windows, he could see the South Tower to his left through the snowfall. The corridor turned and he came to the foot of the Tower, in a small hall with a spiral staircase.

Noting the position of the door to the outside, he began to leap up the stairs, two at a time. He didn't notice the spattered blood he was leaving behind as he went.

Willow and Kepler's rooms were at the very top of the Tower. Boy cursed. The stairs were steep and dark and he couldn't make his legs go fast anymore. But at least Willow should be easy to find—he just had to make it to the top of the staircase.

Suddenly he could go no higher. He put his foot up for the next step and there was none. He stumbled forward and looked about him.

"Willow?" he called, but quietly.

There was no answer. He could see doors in front of him and to the side, three in all.

He looked around. Everyone was in court, or running screaming from the Phantom. He decided he could risk shouting.

"Willow! Are you there?"

Still no answer. There was nothing else for it.

Boy made for the door nearest him and opened it.

Immediately he saw Willow. She was sitting cross-legged on the floor, facing him. As he walked in, she looked up. There was an odd expression on her face, which stopped Boy where he was. Not a look of surprise, or joy, or relief, it was something else, something like fear.

On the floor in front of Willow lay the book, wide open. Boy pointed dumbly.

"Did you . . . ?" he began, but stopped. He didn't know what he was asking.

"Boy . . . ," Willow said, slowly. Then she noticed his arm. "You're hurt!"

"It's all right," said Boy. "It's not too bad. . . ."

"Let me look at it," said Willow, getting to her feet.

Boy shook his head. They were wasting time.

"No!" he cried. "The book. You've read the book!"

Willow stood, like a guilty child, the book at her feet. She looked down at it.

"You've read the book, Willow! Tell me! What does it say?"

"Boy . . . I . . ."

"What did it tell you! Tell me! Or I'll read it myself."

"No!" Willow cried.

Boy strode to where the book lay on the floor. Willow grabbed his arm to stop him and Boy howled with pain. He shoved her away with his good arm and sat down in front of the book.

"No!" cried Willow, and tried to pull the book from Boy.

"Leave me alone!" Boy screamed at her. He pushed at her hands.

"No, Boy! Don't read it! Don't read it! Please!"

Something desperate in Willow's voice struck Boy. He hesitated.

"Why not?" he said, his voice faltering. "Why not? I have to know."

Willow shook her head.

"Maybe it's best you don't. Maybe it's not what you want to hear. Maybe . . ."

"Just tell me, Willow."

"All right. But I want to tell you something first."

Boy waited for her to go on.

"I want you to know. I love you."

Boy showed no emotion, nothing.

"Tell me," he said quietly.

"Valerian's not your father," Willow said. "That's true."

"Then who?" asked Boy.

214

"I don't—"

"Don't tell me you don't know," Boy said.

"No, it's not that. It's just that I don't think you'll want to know. Boy, your father . . . Your father is the emperor. Frederick."

Boy stood, speechless, stunned into silence. A strange look came into his eyes. He smiled, then began to laugh, but stopped just as quickly.

"Don't talk rubbish," he said. "That's ridiculous. . . ."

"I've seen it all, Boy. I've seen it all. Fifteen years ago, the emperor had a son by one of the Beebe women. Sophia."

"Yes, I know. There was something wrong with it. Willow! You weren't there! It's the Phantom, Willow. It's grown into some kind of monster. Maxim let it loose in the court. It's gone crazy, hurting people."

Willow did not seem surprised.

"I know. I saw it in the book. About the strange baby. Frederick had it taken away from Sophia, put it in the dungeons imagining it would die. But it didn't, and even Frederick couldn't bring himself to have his own flesh and blood killed. And he believed he couldn't kill the son the book had foretold. That he would risk Fortune's retribution if he tried to alter the path of Fate by killing the child. But that's not the son I'm talking about, Boy.

"There were twins. One hideous, the other normal. Sophia was horrified by what Frederick had done to her baby, and furious. In revenge, she escaped one night with the healthy child.

"Frederick began to persecute the Beebes. They fell from favor overnight. He confiscated lands and money

215

and removed titles he had bestowed only a little while before. He searched high and low for Sophia.

"Knowing she would be pursued, Sophia tried to hide her tracks. She faked the death of the child. I don't know what happened exactly. I saw . . . in the book . . . I saw the millrace at Linden, and people dragging a woman's body from the water. All I know is that the baby did not die. Somehow, someone must have saved it, and it grew into a boy. A boy who lived on the streets for years, by himself.

"You, Boy. You. You're Frederick's son."

She stopped.

Boy stared through her as if she was a ghost, but if anything it was he who felt like a ghost.

"This can't be true . . . ," he said.

"It's the truth. It may not be the truth you want, but it's the truth all the same."

She put her hand out to him. He didn't push it away but he didn't take it either.

"What did you want to find, Boy? What did you think would make you happy?"

Boy shook his head.

"I don't . . . I don't think . . ." He trailed off, at a loss for words. "I don't know if I wanted to be happy, I just wanted to know."

"And now that you do . . . ?"

"I can't believe it. Frederick . . . my father."

"It's funny. He's so tiny, like you."

"Funny?" cried Boy. "Funny? That's not what—"

"I'm sorry!" Willow said. "I only mean—"

"Never mind," Boy said. "It's just . . . That means that the Phantom . . . is my *brother*."

Willow nodded.

"And Boy, do you know what else it means?"

Boy looked up at her.

"What?"

"When Frederick dies . . . you'll be emperor."

Boy walked over to the window, beyond which was a small balcony. He put his hand to the catch and pushed the narrow glass door open.

"Boy . . . ," said Willow.

He stepped out onto the balcony, and watched the snow. He stood there, staring at the thousands of snow-flakes plummeting to the end of their journey, the end of their dark flight down.

He wanted so much to join them.

But only for a moment. He turned back to Willow.

"Willow," he said.

"Boy?"

"I want to tell you some things too. I love you too. But listen to me. I know who my parents are now. I've got my answers. They're not answers I like very much. Sophia Beebe, who died fifteen years ago. The emperor.

"No. I've been stupid. I've been so desperate to find out, to find the truth, and now that I have, it's all meaningless. It doesn't alter who I am."

Willow smiled. She nodded.

"It doesn't change me," Boy went on. "I was wrong to think it would. I'm just me, Willow. I'm Boy, who lived on the streets, who lived with Valerian, and now who's in love with you. That's who I am."

Willow rushed over to him and they held each other tight.

"And now I know," Boy said, "I don't want anything to do with him. I'm not going to be anyone's emperor. Only you and I know about this—"

"No, Kepler knows."

Boy swore.

"Of course!"

"Kepler knows. That's why he's been trying to get to you."

"What? To get me out of here?"

"No, he wanted to bring you here."

Boy shook his head.

"I don't understand."

"Kepler knows who you are. He's known it ever since he got the book. Ever since he cast your horoscope. And he knew immediately he could use you. He wanted to bring you here, and present you to the emperor. You, his long-lost son. He wasn't quite the unassuming scientist Valerian thought he was. He craved power, having spent years in the wilderness after leaving the Academy. He thought that if he brought you here, and the book too, he'd be show-ered with money, power. He intended to take Maxim's place."

"I can't believe it. That's why he's been so desperate to hang on to me?"

"Yes. It makes sense. Only it happened too soon. Your coming here, I mean. Kepler wanted to do things in his own time. He knew about Maxim, told me how dangerous he is. He was wary of him, and wanted to take things carefully."

"So why did he tell Valerian I was *his* son?"

"It was all he could think of to save you. He knew you were the right age, so he told Valerian the one thing that could save you, and it worked. But all the time he had other plans for you. To bring you here, use you, to get the position of power he wanted."

Boy said nothing, taking time to think it all through. He roused himself, turned to Willow.

"It doesn't matter," he said firmly. "All that matters is that I'm not going be anyone's emperor. We—"

He stopped.

"What?" Willow cried. He was staring past her, over her shoulder.

"Willow!" he choked. He didn't move.

Sensing the fear in Boy's body, Willow turned slowly in his arms, until she saw.

The Phantom.

The Phantom was standing in the doorway of the room. It stared hard at both of them, and lifted one finger to its mouth, licking it. Boy could see blood on the finger, *his* blood.

The beast took a step forward, and in the lamplight, Boy could see its face clearly for the first time. Now at last he knew what it was that had horrified him the night he had run into the Phantom in the palace tunnels. What it was about the thing's eyes. It was that they were his own.

His brother. His mutated monster of a brother.

Boy and Willow waited for the attack, yet still the Phantom paused. It seemed not to have noticed Willow at all, but kept its eyes fixed on Boy alone.

Eye to eye, their gazes met, Boy and beast. Boy looked deep into those eyes. Beyond the tragic face, beyond the watery gray film across the eyes themselves, and further, he looked into the Phantom's mind.

Were there thoughts there? Real thoughts? Or just impulses, to kill, to eat, to run?

There had to be more to his brother than that. Boy took a deep breath, and smiled.

He stepped forward, and put his hand out to his brother.

The Phantom looked at Boy, put his head on one side, like a dog considering something. He licked the blood on his fingers once more, and moved slowly forward.

There was a clattering of feet on the steps, and Kepler burst into the room.

"No!" he shrieked, and flung himself at the Phantom from behind.

The Phantom was thrown to the floor, but pulled Kepler down with him, knocking over the table with the lamp. The lamp shattered and oil spread across the floor, a moment later catching fire and exploding. The room was lit only by the flames flickering up the side of the overturned table.

Willow screamed.

Boy screamed too.

"No!"

But it was too late. The Phantom rose and attacked Kepler, who had come armed with a knife.

Boy watched horrified as the two figures struggled to their feet. They stumbled as one body, and backed into the burning table, which caught on the Phantom's rags instantly. It shrieked with pain and lashed out at Kepler, dashing him backward onto the balcony.

"No! Stop it! Stop it!" Boy cried.

The Phantom lurched after Kepler, who was getting to his feet. The Phantom hit him hard in a crazed attack that sent them both hurtling toward the balustrade. Boy and Willow shrieked as both figures plunged over the balcony.

Boy rushed out and was in time to see the burning figures plunge like a comet through the snowy night to the flags of the courtyard below. They were still.

"No!" he cried, heedless that the whole palace could hear him. "No!"

Willow hurried to his side and looked down. Then she turned and buried her face in Boy's neck.

Boy put his arm around her.

"Come on," he said. His voice sounded calm, and strong.

Willow looked up at him.

"It's time we left," he said, "but there's one more thing we have to do first."

Willow nodded.

The book.

They both turned to where it lay on the floor, a few feet from the burning table. The book that had caused so much pain and death.

Together they made their way over to the book, and knelt by it. What they did next was not easy. It seemed to be radiating hostility toward them, as if it knew. They began to shake as they lifted the thing between them, the book suddenly feeling much heavier than ever before.

"Maybe . . . ," began Willow, but Boy shook his head.

"No," he said, powerfully. "It's the end."

They opened it and fanned its pages into the flames of the burning table.

"Die," said Boy under his breath. "Die."

The flames seemed to lick around its pages and cover, but they would not take. It was as if it was impervious to fire.

"It won't burn!" cried Willow. "It won't!"

They watched, terrified, as if they'd been caught trying to kill someone. The book sat in the flames, and they grew more afraid.

"It won't burn!" cried Willow, again.

"No," Boy said. "Look!"

He was right.

The book hissed, like green birch logs. It crackled, and seethed, and spat spots of flame at them, but it was catching.

"Burn!" Boy shouted. "Burn!"

The spitting got worse and Boy and Willow backed away as finally the ancient, stained, grimy, ink-littered pages began to burn. Page by page caught, a lovely orange flame spreading across it, running the paper into blackness, before vaporizing as hot carbon dust.

With each page that went Boy and Willow felt their hearts grow lighter, and their fears recede.

The cover had caught now, and the leather was giving off noxious curls of stinking smoke that made their eyes water.

"Die," Boy whispered. "Go."

Willow held Boy's hand.

"It's time we went too," she said.

So they did.

3

Boy and Willow walked through the City streets. It felt to them both as if they had been away for years, although it was only a matter of days. So much had happened.

The snow was falling still, but it seemed possible that it was easing. Rumors of food shortages were spreading, though, and people wore grim expressions as they went about their business on the bitter January morning.

They'd risked spending the night at Kepler's house, having fled the palace. It had been easier to escape than they might have imagined, with chaos still spreading from the court, people dead or wounded by the Phantom, guards searching for Maxim, and Frederick barking away atop his throne. In all this madness, they had been able to leave the South Tower unobserved. They'd run along through the various palace courtyards until they found themselves by one of the outer walls.

They still had to get out somehow, but it was the snow that had saved them, after all, the irony of which was not lost on Boy. He had yearned for forgetting all through the snowfall, and in the end it *was* the snow that had saved them, though in a much more mundane way. From the top of the palace wall they saw that a huge drift of snow had formed between the outer wall and the bank from which it rose. Holding hands, they had dared to jump, and tumbled down the thick, sloping snowdrift as gently as if they had landed on a goose-feather quilt.

As they left the palace behind, and crossed the river, they saw that the Old South Tower was alight, flames shooting up into the snow-speckled night sky around them, sparks dancing upward as the snowflakes fluttered down.

"That's the end of the book," Willow said.

"Yes," Boy replied. "It will cause no more suffering."

Willow smiled and held Boy's hand. She looked into his eyes.

"What is it?" she asked.

"People were wrong about him," Boy said. "Maybe he wasn't just a monster. Maybe if someone had looked after him . . ."

"Your brother?"

Boy nodded.

Willow thought of something else.

"He tried to save you, you know. Perhaps he did genuinely care for you."

She meant Kepler.

"No," said Boy, shaking his head. "He only wanted me, needed me alive, to get what he wanted."

"Oh!" cried Willow, and turned, grabbing Boy's hands.

"What?" asked Boy. "What is it?"

"The book!" said Willow. "There was something else I saw."

A look of alarm crossed Boy's face.

"What?" he asked. "What did you see?"

"Your name!"

"No!" cried Boy. "No! Don't tell me! I don't want to know."

"But, Boy . . . ," Willow said.

"No! I don't want to know. I am Boy, that's all. That's all I want to be."

"But, Boy, you don't understand. What I saw. In the book, I saw Sophia, your mother, escaping with you. It was all so quick. She knew she had to escape with you, so she fled the castle, and headed out to the countryside. But she hadn't even had time to give you a name."

"So I never had a name at all?" said Boy. He seemed calm; there was no anger, no pain in him now.

"No," said Willow. "No. Except, in the book, I heard your mother talking to you, all the time, as she hurried along with you in her arms. Talking to you, talking, talking, hushing your cries, blessing you with love, and all she called you was Boy, my lovely Boy, my darling little Boy. Boy."

Boy moved closer to Willow. She pulled him toward her, looked deep into his eyes.

"Boy. That's what she called you," she said. "That's your real name after all. Boy."

She put her arms round him, and held him fast until his tears were gone.

Now, in the dim light of the following morning, they were leaving. They'd found a decent stash of money in Kepler's study, and had packed clothes and blankets and some other valuables into two large bags. It was all they had, but it was more than either of them had ever owned before, and they knew it would be enough.

"They probably will never come looking for you," Willow said. "There's too much confusion there."

"I know," said Boy, "but that's not the only reason we're leaving."

"To think, Frederick was so desperate for an heir, and there you were, right under his nose. Now there's only you and me who know."

She laughed.

"What?" asked Boy.

"Just think. You're the heir to the empire. And if we ever tried to tell anyone, no one would believe us!"

She stopped.

"Are you sure, Boy? Are you sure? You'd be very rich. Powerful!"

Boy looked at her.

"In that madhouse? With those lunatics? No, Willow, we don't need that kind of money or power. We just need enough to get by, and each other. And I think we'll do that best somewhere else."

They walked on, heading for the City gates.

Their route took them past St. Valentine's Fountain. They both smiled, but remained silent until it was far behind them.

"But where are we going to go?" Willow asked, not for the first time, as they reached the Northern Gate.

They stood on the threshold.

Behind them lay the huge, rambling, decrepit, awful, wonderful City, more or less all they had ever known. Their whole past lay in its maw. Ahead of them lay nothing they could see, but the emptiness and whiteness of a snow-laden, unknown future.

"I don't know," said Boy.

"We could go to Linden. After all, you're a Beebe, sort of."

"After what we did to their church? I don't think so. Anyway, I think I've got it wrong all these years. Wanting to have a past. To go back to Linden would be to make the same mistake. So let's go and find a future, shall we?"

They pulled their coats around them, and walked out into the pure white countryside, and as they did so, the snow began to ease. A small break opened in the clouds above them, and a weak but warming winter sun shone down on their path.

Epilogue

Midnight in the Imperial Court of Emperor Frederick III. The court is empty.

The emperor sits on his throne, brooding.

"Maxim!" he calls, in his high, pathetic voice. "Dammit, Maxim, where are you?"

He waves a hand in the darkness, and flakes of his ancient skin drift up into the gloom.

"Maxim, I need your help! I don't think you understand. Sometimes I really think you're trying to kill me! Do you hear me? You have no idea how difficult it is for me. You should help me more, Maxim. You really should understand. I need a solution, Maxim. Yes! And you're going to find it for me.

"Maxim, are you listening? Maxim! Maxim!"

The emperor calls out in the darkness, in his madness, forgetting, forgetting.

Forgetting that things have changed, forgetting what has happened, forgetting what he's decreed.

* * *

And far beneath the emperor, chained to a rough stone wall at the bottom of the dark flight of stairs where the emperor's sad son used to lurk, lies Maxim, blinking in the darkness.

> *So dance, my dears, dance,*
> *Before you take the dark flight down.*

About the Author

MARCUS SEDGWICK's first book, *Floodland*, was hailed as "a dazzling debut from a new writer of exceptional talent" and won the Branford Boase Award for a best first novel. Since then, he has written *Witch Hill*, which was nominated for an Edgar Allan Poe Award for Best Young Adult Novel; *The Dark Horse*, which was short-listed for the Guardian Award for Children's Fiction, the Carnegie Medal and the Blue Peter Book Award and was a *School Library Journal* Best Book of the Year; and *The Book of Dead Days*, the prequel to *The Dark Flight Down*.

Marcus Sedgwick has worked in children's publishing in England for ten years; before that, he was a bookseller. In addition to writing, he does stone carvings, etchings and woodcuts. He lives in Sussex and has a young daughter, Alice.